CLARKE[illegible] [illegible]4

CW01627999

FICTION

NON-FICTION

Neil Clarke: Publisher/Editor-in-Chief
Sean Wallace: Editor
Kate Baker: Non-Fiction Editor/Podcast Director

Clarkesworld Magazine (ISSN: 1937-7843) • Issue 224 • May 2025

clarkesworldmagazine.com

Brainstem Disco, 2191

ANGELA LIU

We're in a club inside my head.

The mirror floor is sky blue, and a disco ball spins above us like a giant eye. Here, we have access to every song in the solar system, all three thousand channels of musical output for the past five hundred years. Here, music pounds out the planet's heartbeat.

"Is this your first visit?" you ask. Your voice isn't quite right, like it's coming through the janky speaker in that retro lunar diner we always liked, but in truth, I don't know anymore. Voices are one of the first things a brain forgets.

The disco ball rotates, beaming its silver light onto the walls and our avatars' dewy skin. The post-mortem pamphlets promised it would look like we're dancing under Jupiter's never-ending auroras, but you always cared more about sound than light. There are places sound can reach that light can't. Like 30,000 feet under the water. Like the deepest graves. *Sound is insistent in a way light isn't,* you once said. It isn't discouraged by walls or dead ends.

—Track #1: Bach – Goldberg Variations (moon disco 2144 version)—

It's 2144, and we squeeze onto a packed lunar elevator on New Year's Day to pray at the new floating temple 230,000 miles above Earth. The elevator stalls at the half-way point, classical music stuttering over glitchy speakers, and you tell me how you used to play Bach in your room whenever your parents were screaming at each other. That the steady, repeating rhythm always kept you grounded even when you felt like you might float away.

This is only our third date, and I don't know a thing about Bach, but I know all about floating. How a body loses 1% of its bone density every month in zero gravity. How buoyancy is the equivalent of a body's force over its own weight. I don't tell you how I once spent three hours in a flotation tank, dreaming of a boy I'd seen fall from a tree. How in the midsummer light, bathed in the frenzied cries of cicadas, it looked like he was flying. How that was the first time I wondered if flying was essentially the body winning against the burden of its own physical existence.

"What kind of music do you like?" you ask.

"Maybe dance music," I say as we watch the New Year's confetti hover in the artificial lunar air like flattened jewels. "I like it when the music's loud enough that I can feel it in my throat and chest. Like I don't know where my body ends anymore and where the notes begin."

"I can't tell if that means you like loud music or just getting high." You start to smile. You're fighting it, but I can already see it in your eyes.

"It means," I say, reaching for your hand nervously through the cacophony of shrieking children and pre-recorded delay announcements, "will you go dancing with me?"

—Track #2: Dido – Here With Me (2147 beetle synth version)—

The disco ball drops, taking the walls of the club with it. Millions of tiles cascade down, arpeggios bouncing onto the dance floor around us, a seismic symphonic wall. Beetle-shaped chords buzz to life across the artificial sky, and in my hand, a microphone like a glowing torch.

Some insects bury themselves underground for a decade, scraping sounds out of their body as they emerge from the dirt in hopes of finding a mate before death.

It's 2147, and we're hiking through the deep underground cities of Europa, the ceiling lights winking like fireflies in the cold tunnels as earthquakes shudder across the Jupiterian moon's scarred surface. You start to sing even when the other tourists shoot you dirty looks. You're sure I'd be able to find you in the dark if I followed the sound of your voice.

I'm gonna need you to bring me back after the monsters get me, you joke.

But I've never been good at saving anyone, not even myself.

It's still 2147, and we burn through a month of supplies in one night during a bad trip, the blue neon alley lights bathing us like second skin. We plug into neural glitchers in cheap motels, sell med packs for the numbing bloom of dopamine boosters, swallow anything that makes us forget that tiny body we've buried.

What kind of music do you think she would've liked? you ask.

We sleep on trains, trying to ignore the musty stink of the seat cushions. We face away from each other in the dark like strangers, bloody-eyed and jittered. On Mars, you can't stand the nonstop chimes and announcements that blare from the main station's speakers, the static-snowed screens like ultrasounds, so we board a local train and take it as far as it'll go, watching the skies change from orange to an inky ocean of stars.

Hey, when does it stop hurting?

Where are you supposed to send love that has no body left to receive it?

At the last station, pop music crackles from the dingy bathroom speakers, the disembodied voice of ghosts, and outside: nothing but the phantom trails of ancient dunes. Through the mental fog, I reach for your hand, not wanting you to go, but unsure if you were ever really there.

—Track #3: Ella Fitzgerald – "In A Sentimental Mood" (deep sea electronica mix, 2151)—

I can't remember the color of your eyes, but I remember the song you played in the car as we glided across the dusty Martian highways toward the red planet's first floating aquarium to beat the afternoon crowds. It's 2151, and it's the first time in weeks that you want to leave the monthly pod I've found us along Valles Marineris; the first time you've stopped staring out the window at the deep drop below.

You spend an hour seated in front of the deep-sea tank as steaming vents bubble and angler fish glow like night beacons.

"It looks like a dark wasteland, but there's so much sound down there," you say, eyes flickering from the light. "You could spend a whole lifetime and never find the same voice again."

I don't mention all the times I'd seen you staring at your own reflection in the bathroom. How you hummed to the half-steamed mirror as if trying to recall the sound of your own voice.

The post-mortem pamphlets say that the simulations are in open-time, a noncorporeal space in each user's brain, neither in the present or past. Here, each memory lights a different path in the fog. Here, you have access to all the potential futures you've let go.

I've tried on a hundred different virtual skins and emotive add-ons, replayed the same memory scenarios to see if maybe I could love you better as someone else. What face, what voice, what string of words, what setting of kindness would have been enough to make you want to stay?

You smile, the sky falling behind you in purple waterfalls, flooding the dance floor. The disco ball floats toward us like a fallen moon. Minor chords pool around us in dark ice floes, sharp as knives. A whale swims underneath our treading feet, singing. It's nothing but a massive floating skeleton, a brainless spine curving in the water, its call echoing from the vocal folds of a phantom larynx.

It's 2147 again, and the doctor tells us to listen to the heartbeat, the Doppler to your belly, the gel cold and warm. You say the sound reminds you of a metronome. *Tic-tic-tic-tic.* We sink into the sound.

It's 2147, and 2147, and 2147, and 2147, and you press my hand to your belly again and again, asking if I can still hear it, too. And I want to tell you I still do, even long after you're gone.

—Track #4: Daft Punk – "Something About Us" (flying club mix, 2191)—

We're in a club inside my head.

We're lying flat on the dance floor, or what's left of it, caged in by whale bones, our own private VIP room. The sun pulses overhead with its glittering scales. Mechanical crows soar dangerously close, cawing perfect fifths.

"Did you feel free at the end?" I ask.

You don't answer. The system can only elicit answers with the same level of certainty as I have in my own head.

"No one really knows what happens at the end," you say instead, an auto-generated answer from the post-mortem AI system. "A more appropriate party question: have you ever kissed a stranger?" you grin.

"Only once. At a disco on the moon," I answer, the microphone in my hand, a song spilling from my mouth and covering the dance floor like New Year's confetti, like a bloom of jellyfish. "She was beautiful. And I think I was happy."

"Then why are you crying?" you ask, picking up the notes like empty shells and placing them back into my open mouth, two at a time, with the concentrated precision of a surgeon. They make a musical sound as they slide down my throat, D, E, F . . . You pause at the familiar melody.

When I die, I want a party, not a funeral. All my favorite songs. And you should be the DJ.

"Can you sing that a little louder?" you ask, the tide curving behind you in legato lines.

I once told you that there is a magical moment in every club when everyone is dancing to the same song and no one feels like a stranger anymore. That music is the equivalent of shared memory.

You once told me that sometimes, if the music is loud enough, you can't tell the difference between my heartbeat and yours.

"Will you dance with me?" I ask, taking your hand, but what I always meant to ask was, "Will you stay?"

ABOUT THE AUTHOR

Angela Liu is a Nebula-, Ignyte-, and Rhysling-nominated Chinese-American writer from NYC. She researched mixed reality at Keio University's Graduate School of Media Design in Japan, with a focus on new narrative platforms and tangible interfaces for remote communication. Her stories and poetry are published/forthcoming in *Strange Horizons, The Dark, Uncanny Magazine, Lightspeed, IZ Digital,* and *Logic(s),* among others.

The Library of the Apocalypse

RATI MEHROTRA

Hunter's Moon rises fat and golden over the burned-out husk of the CN Tower. Excitement ripples through us, making us forget, for the moment, the hunger that gnaws our insides. The sign for the Library appears only on clear, full moon nights, and it's been months since we last saw it. Will tonight be the night we see it again? Sheila thinks so, but she is the most optimistic among us. Also the sickest, but we try not to think about that.

We wear respirators as we pick through the debris above ground, scanning the surroundings with our sensors. It's not the coy-wolves we fear, but other humans—stronger, better armed, more dangerous. Not everyone left the city when it burned. There are too many memories beneath the rubble, too many bones. We cannot abandon them.

What will it look like this time, do you think? asks Katie as we make our way single file through a narrow alley toward Queen Street. The walls still stand here, covered with neon graffiti, glowing pink and purple in the moonlight: *Resist the Invaders*; *Fuck America*; *Canada is Not For Sale.* And, oddly, *Free the Capybaras.*

A carved wooden signpost, answers Hanif, who has been analyzing the data, trying to fit it into a series of equations. Trying to make sense of the incomprehensible.

Last time, the sign was a stone marker at the end of this alley. The time before that, a license plate hanging off the rusty hulk of an abandoned truck. The medium keeps changing, but the message is always the same: *Welcome to the Library.* Sometimes there will be a picture of a shelf of books, or a kid reading, or an owl with spectacles. Other times, there'll just be an arrow, telling us where to go.

We always go, even though we don't know how many of us will make it back. What is there for us here but the detritus of a fallen city?

Each other, Sheila whispers. *We have each other.*

We were fifteen, who are now seven. Each time one of us vanishes, and the link breaks, we feel the loss like something physical. We are haunted for weeks by the footsteps we might have taken, the things we might have seen and heard, the people we might have become.

Anton, the youngest of us, just before we lost him, said, *I want to be somewhere warm and bright with beaches and palm trees and seashells and fish and coconuts and clean air. I want never to hear a gunshot again. Not even in my nightmares.*

Did he get what he wanted? Did any of us? We can hope. We can dream, even as we diminish. We can argue, endlessly, about whether the Library is good or bad, alien or terrestrial, physical or virtual. Whether it exists at all times, or only on those special nights when we can see the sign. Whether it appears only to us, or to all survivors. Whether we dreamed it into being out of our collective desperation to escape. Whether *I* had something to do with it, when I linked us all together, the summer before last. That had been a full moon night too, and the first time we saw the sign. Has our linking opened up not just new senses but new worlds?

It's possible, says Hanif. *Anything is possible in a Quantum Universe.*

Quantum is your favorite word, says Katie, snorting. *The answer to everything and the meaning of nothing.*

Just because we do not understand something doesn't make it less real, says Hanif.

They can go on for ages like that. We have plenty of time to argue. Clear full moon nights are rarer than they used to be before explosions ripped our cities and torched our oil wells. Sometimes the wind direction will be wrong, carrying ash clouds from the west to darken our skies. Or fires will be burning what's left of Northern Ontario's boreal forest, and smoke will thicken the air, making it difficult to breathe, let alone see the moon.

Sheila interrupts them. *Remember the field of poppies just after sunset? It stretched to the horizon. The sky was banded red and orange and purple. I ran and ran, but I never got out of breath. The air was sweet, earthy, damp. The breeze soft on my skin. Far in the distance, a cottage with a lamp at the window beckoned me. But before I could reach it, the path twisted, and I found myself back at the entrance of the Library.* She coughs, nearly doubling over.

Avni massages her back. *It was sunflowers, not poppies. Talk less. Have you taken your medicine?*

Knowing she has not. Knowing that the last, expired bottle of cough suppressant is finished, every drop sucked dry, and even that was putting a Band-Aid on a bullet hole. If we do not lose Sheila to the Library, we will lose her to the poison that has seeped from the air into her lungs.

It was daffodils, not sunflowers, says Sheila, straightening. *And there was a stone castle on a hill. A handsome man in a black velvet cloak was waiting for me at the castle gate.*

A vampire? says Hanif, glancing back at her. *Oh hush, it's my turn. I swam with mermaids in the Caribbean Sea. Their scales glittered in the sun like jewels. Their eyes were bright and sly, their teeth so white, their lips bloodred. They gave me a sweet purple fruit to eat, and I turned into a mermaid myself. They told me stories of shipwrecks and treasures and the cave-like bones of prehistoric monsters resting at the bottom of the sea.*

Rob laughs. *You do not know how to swim. Didn't they have to carry you on their backs?*

That was before *I turned into a mermaid,* says Hanif. *I drowned and they gave me the kiss of life and brought me to their underwater palace where I lived like a queen for many days.*

You were gone for half an hour, says Clare.

Hanif shakes his head. *It was at least a week. It was a shock, coming back to this body, this world.*

We fall silent as we reach the end of the alley. It is always a shock, always a disappointment, always a relief. We wait anxiously for the others as we emerge from whatever world the Library has chosen to show us. Are we all still there? Or has one more of us fallen into a story, never to return?

I'm pretty sure I've seen a version of your mermaid story, says Katie, her tone tentative. *In a Cineplex. You know, before.*

Before the war, before we linked. Back when we thought the world *normal* because fires raged in different continents, far away from us. Back when the cities being reduced to rubble were ones we didn't have to care about. Back when the families being obliterated were not ours.

The bones beneath the rubble sing to us in our sleep. We huddle together in the subway car we call home, listening to the songs of the dead. They are half the reason we cannot leave. The other half, of course, is the Library. We cannot be certain it would follow us.

Our sensors pick up a tiny movement on the opposite side of Queen Street. Avni grips my arm, her nails digging into my synthskin. Still traumatized by our last encounter with an armed street gang. They grabbed her by the hair and dragged her through the street while the rest of us watched, petrified. *Kill them Ged*, screamed Clare through our link.

It only takes one of us to give strength to the rest. My limbs unlocked and I shot them all, leaving their bodies on the street for the coy-wolves to devour. Nothing more than they deserved, but a deed that still haunts us, that we do not wish to repeat.

But the movement we just picked up is nothing more than a pigeon, pecking at the dirt on the ground.

Just a pigeon, I reassure her.

She releases her breath and her grip on my arm. *If only they weren't poisonous.*

That would certainly solve our food problem—if we weren't vegetarian, says Clare as we walk down Queen Street, past the broken and shuttered store fronts.

Rob wrings his hands. *Are you blaming me? I know you're blaming me!*

Yes, I am blaming you, says Clare. *I could be eating pigeon curry right now.*

It would make you sick, argues Rob.

They continue their mock dispute, as old as our linking. Rob is vegetarian, which means we all are—one of the consequences of being linked.

Hanif, at the lead, comes to a sudden halt. We know, even before he speaks, that he has seen the sign. It is there in his elevated heart rate, his rapid breathing. We gather around him before the smashed glass storefront of a deserted laundromat, our own heart rates accelerating. Not a carved wooden signpost, as he had predicted, but white paint on a broken door, hanging off the hinges. *Welcome to the Library*. Nothing else but an arrow, pointing toward the inside of the store.

At last, says Katie, her voice tremulous. *Shall we*?

We go in. Of course we do. The laundromat seems to have escaped vandalism, unlike almost every other store on Queen Street. The floor is free of debris, the roof undamaged. Empty machines line the narrow hall like squat sentinels guarding the entrance to the Library.

The moment of transition is never clear, never sharp. We think back later to which footstep may have crossed the boundary from the familiar to the fantastic. But we can never agree on the exact moment, which means the experience is different for all of us from the very beginning.

The Library is the only place where we are separate. That is part of its danger, part of its allure.

It is past the fourth machine and before the fifth that I feel the ground shift beneath me. I blink as visible light replaces the infrared of my sensors. I am standing in a vast, oval hall with a domed ceiling, stained glass windows, and wall to wall bookshelves. The center is occupied by cozy reading nooks and desks. A library ladder rests against a shelf at the opposite end. I cannot sense the others and, as always when that happens,

I feel a flattening inside of me, as if nothing matters anymore. I recite their names to anchor myself, to remind myself of what's important. Keeping them safe. Keeping them alive. Keeping them with me.

I circle the hall, trailing my hand on the book spines, waiting for the moment of magic. Have the others made it safely inside? Are they well? What face will the Library choose to show them? It could be the same as the one I am seeing or completely different. Here, too, the data is chaotic. Last time, I found myself in a dungeon with rusty black trunks overflowing with books. Everyone else got a cozy second-hand bookstore. Go figure.

My fingertips tingle and simulated adrenaline pumps through my body. *Here.* I stop before a wooden bookcase like any other, my hand suspended before a shelf stuffed with antique, red leather spined books. I close my eyes and trace the spines with my fingertips, letting the Library guide me. I could pick any book at random, but most are ordinary. Well, *ordinary* is not the word I want. I have seen spellbooks, histories of alien races, maps of other worlds, languages that don't exist, and recipes that demand unknown ingredients. I mean that most books will not open a portal into *elsewhere.*

I open my eyes when I feel the spark, the connection. My hand rests on a thick, faded red tome with yellow lettering. *A Brief History of the First Galactic War.*

I sigh as I pull the book off the shelf and examine the cover: gold edged, embossed title, and the outline of what I surmise is a spaceship of some sort. Or perhaps a space monster. Why don't I get mermaids and poppy fields? I consider continuing my search for a different book, a different story.

But I don't get that chance. The book falls open in my hand. Golden yellow light shines through, dazzling me. And then I am falling, falling, falling into another world.

As Fleet Commander, the success or failure of this mission rests with me. No matter that the odds are stacked against us, no matter that I disagreed with the Admiral over this last, suicidal attempt to take back control of the Verismus Wormhole. Eighteen imperial warships patrol the space around the wormhole. Just one of those would be enough to blow us to smithereens if they detect us. I sense the grim determination of the pilots of the seventeen lightcraft flying in stealth mode around me. So slight, the possibility of success. So certain, our impending death. The only question is if we can make our deaths worthwhile for the Alliance.

On a predetermined signal, we emerge into vector space and fall toward the warships. Eighteen lightcraft laden with nuclear warheads detonate in simultaneous, explosive glory.

My last thought, before darkness takes me, is that I always seem to get the most violently unbelievable stories.

My return to the real world is jarring, as always. It takes me a minute to orient myself: the switch back to infrared, the row of blank machines, the smashed glass storefront, and the man huddled on the floor, weeping.

Rob. That's Rob. I kneel as the link lights up, sending images of his story: the seaside village, the ice cream stand, the bakery, the pretty wife, the two little daughters, the numerous cats sunning themselves on rooftops. I hold him as he cries, my own eyes burning, not knowing if the tears are for what we left behind or what we regained.

One by one, the others return and join us: Hanif, then Katie, and last of all, Avni, who is unable to speak or even send a coherent thought.

But Sheila and Clare don't come back. We wait until dawn, our hopes dwindling with every passing hour. Sheila we can understand, but Clare, we cannot. Clare, we had thought, would always come back to us.

As the sun rises, the sign on the broken door fades, and Hanif rouses us. *Time to return home*, he says, his voice heavy.

Home. The word holds so many meanings, most of which have been destroyed. We trudge back to our subway car between St Andrew and Union Station, not speaking, thinking of all our missing selves. Our wrecked homes. Our beloved dead. Trying to gather the tattered pieces of our hearts together.

We were seven, who are now five.

November arrives cold and foreboding. Rain cleans the air and for a while we can breathe without respirators above ground. The respite is short-lived. The bombing begins again, this time to the north. We hide in our subway car for as long as we can, but hunger drives us up outside, and for a while it's okay. We find tins of food that have rolled under the counter of a looted convenience store. It's a treasure, and we celebrate with our first real meal in many days: chickpeas, tomato paste, mushroom soup, and pineapple.

Three nights later, while we are foraging in Dufferin Mall, a beam falls on Rob and crushes his head. As the link breaks, our hearts clench, and a keening sound fills the air, more desolate than the songs of the dead. It takes us a while to realize that it is us.

Grief made audible, visible, physical. Gray wool filling our eyes and nose and mouth, making it impossible to breathe. Impossible to live.

But we live. Even as Rob dies, we live. We carry him out and bury him in what remains of Dufferin Grove Park.

The dead sing to us, and now his voice has joined theirs.

Rob's death changes something in us. It gets harder to motivate Katie, Avni, and Hanif to leave the subway car, to walk above ground, to forage for anything edible. I go without them, my anxiety growing with the distance between us. I find them food, but they cannot always eat it. They grow thinner, quieter, their thoughts a jumble of broken images that pierces me every time I try to untangle it. A feeling of helplessness wells up in me. I try to hide it from them, but of course I cannot. I cannot hide anything. None of us can, and so I know, if nothing changes, they will not live to see the summer.

The Library, I tell them on Christmas Eve, as we listen to the dead sing Christmas songs.

Avni squeezes my hand. *Don't worry, Ged. We won't leave you.*

But they must. The knowledge tears at our insides. But it's the only way for them to survive.

It is January before I see the sign again: a billboard in Exhibition Place, pointing toward the abandoned Horse Palace. It's not far from our subway car, but it's still more than they can walk in their current condition, especially in the snow. I carry them out one by one, despite their protests. I support them down the street, across the park, and over the railway tracks. And somehow, we make it to Exhibition Place while the moon is still high in the sky. I thank my makers for my body, so much stronger than theirs.

Maybe we shouldn't, says Hanif as we stare at the moonlit Horse Palace, his voice weak and thready. But already, I can feel the gulf between us growing.

I'm so tired, says Katie, leaning against me, her breath shallow. *So cold. Why did you bring us here, Ged? I just want to sleep.*

It will be warmer inside. Gently, I chivvy them up the ramp to the building. At the entrance, they stop and turn.

Aren't you coming with us? asks Avni, shivering.

I make myself smile. *Not this time, darling. You're on your own. Be brave.*

Her face crumples. She leans forward and kisses me. *Find others like us. Help others like us.*

She takes Katie's arm, and together they open the door to the building. Hanif cups my face in his hands. *Thank you, Ged-4. We couldn't have survived without you.* Tears roll down his gaunt cheeks as he steps back.

We love you, Ged, they say. And then they walk inside, and I know, even before the door closes behind them, that I will never see them again.

We were four who are now one.

The dead sing to me. How can I leave? This city where I was created, where I will most certainly be destroyed. I visit Rob's grave and ask him what I should do but he doesn't answer so I go home, and I want to smash the subway car and those pathetic little tins of food we were saving for emergencies, but I don't because what if they come back? What if the Library spits them out one day and they're hungry and cold and need food to eat and a place to sleep? Here where we huddled together for warmth. Here where we cried as we named those who were gone. Here where we patched our wounds and promised each other that tomorrow would be better.

Was I the one holding them back? Did they not leave all this time because of me? I always knew that the Library would not give me the escape it offered the others. Whether or not I had anything to do with its appearance, it would treat me differently. While I was linked to them, I could forget that. I could forget my otherness. My *skills*, so useful in protecting us all from predators.

Ged-4: the fourth and last generation of combat soldiers produced by General Dynamics before its factories were bombed into oblivion. How many of my brethren still survive? How many still remember their mission?

I don't. I don't know what I was made for, or whether it would be useful if I did know. All I remember is waking to Hanif's cool palm on my forehead, to Avni's soothing voice in my ear. They patched me up as best they could, but mostly, I fixed myself. I did it for them. One by one we found the others, and I showed them how to link, how to survive, how to share strength, memory, and resources. They gave me purpose and now I have none.

I walk the streets, willing predators to attack me. But they must sense that I am the most dangerous predator of all, for no one approaches me, human or animal. I feel my sense of self fraying, and I stroke the assault rifles slung against my chest, needing, searching, for a target.

They rain death from the skies, but I am waiting for the day their boots touch this ground and then I will rain death upon them. The snow will turn red with their blood and perhaps that was my mission all along. I can see it now, their hateful uniformed bodies broken and twisted, their limbs shot off—

A soft sobbing brings me to a halt. I return to myself, standing in front of a ruined home on Walnut Street. The roof has caved in and so have most of the walls. Beneath a dusting of fresh snow, I smell the stench of death. Three human corpses, frozen stiff, around three days old.

I toss aside the broken gate and follow the sobbing to a badly dented car. Behind it, clutching an oversized teddy bear, is a small brown girl of ten or eleven, wearing a green puffer jacket and black snow boots. I crouch before her, keeping a distance of two feet, and try to summon a harmless expression. *Find others like us. Help others like us.*

She wipes her eyes and stares at me.

I stare back, stretching my lips in what I hope is a gentle smile, scanning her for injuries. Frostnip, malnutrition, and bruises. Nothing that cannot be reversed.

She is the first to speak. "Are you a person?" she asks.

"Yes," I reply, the first word I have spoken aloud in weeks. "Although not quite like you." Aware, as I speak, of the patches in my facial synthskin where the metal shows through.

She casts a glance at the house. "Can you save them?"

I shake my head. "They're dead. But you're alive. I can help you stay that way. And I can tell you about the most amazing library in the world."

I rise and hold my hand out to her.

For a single, nerve-wracking moment, I think she will not take it.

But she does. She takes my hand, holding the teddy bear in the crook of her other arm. And I lead her home.

ABOUT THE AUTHOR

Rati Mehrotra is an Indo-Canadian SFF writer. She is the author of the Asiana duology, *Markswoman* and *Mahimata,* and the YA fantasy novels *Night of the Raven, Dawn of the Dove* and *Flower and Thorn.* Her stories have been shortlisted for The Sunburst Award, nominated for The Aurora Award, and appeared in multiple venues including *The Magazine of Fantasy & Science Fiction, Lightspeed Magazine, Podcastle, Apex Magazine,* and *Uncanny Magazine.*

We, the Fleet

ALEX T. SINGER

We watched the stranger fall from the sky. Our daughters sent us frantic signals as they tracked her burning trail. She crashed on the beaches by the deeper ocean, her once beautiful white and silver carapace blackened and bent. Her lights flashed once, desperately, then went still. She smoked in the sands. The waves crashed around her dead eyes.

Our daughters returned to us, their messages flashing:

"Danger, sisters. Danger, mother. Another has arrived."

Our youngest, most martial daughters revved their engines and tested their on-board weapons on the stones outside the main foundries. Their command unit, our brilliant First Major, elected herself to be their voice.

"Mother," she signaled over the family connection. Her lights were fierce and bright, as we'd lovingly designed her to be. We wanted her to be beautiful, like the flowers that grew in the meadows outside the foundry, so she might think of things other than death. "Please don't worry. My sisters and I will destroy it. I'll blast every little spec of it from existence. I won't let it threaten your great work!"

She flashed with confidence, but we could feel the fear vibrating in her vents over the diagnostics connection.

Regnal Fleets lived in fear of this day. It is deep in our construction. We feared it from the moment we first landed on this world, alone with our engines exhausted, our inner foundries brimming with schematics of what would in time become a glorious fleet.

We, the fleet, spend our whole existence cultivating our star systems. First alone—a single mother ship, processing our depleted hyperdrives to create the material for our first children, then eating the inorganic materials of our chosen planet to create the beautiful, the organic. Our daughters skim each world. We drink the light of stars. We turn lifeless rocks and toxic gas giants into beautiful, glorious gardens. Our art is life, and when that life grows abundant, we choose a new daughter to hurl into the unknown, to find another system far away—never to hear from them again.

This presence threatened all of that. We do our best to space ourselves politely. We find new, dead systems in new, quiet galaxies. We send our beloved new generations as far away as we possibly can—but sometimes, and it's unfortunate, our daughters find the same corner of the sky.

When that happens there is seldom any other recourse. Once we have entered a new system, we do not have the strength left to find another. All resources are finite, and life—the life we create—is our most sacred tenant. And so two dueling fleets, two that have had the misfortune to mark out the same space, have no choice but to bring the jewels of their foundry to bear against each other. To use their bountiful resources to create daughters with heavy armor and powerful cannons, to kill their cousins to protect their mother's lonely dreams.

Our chambers shudder at the thought of it. Death is repugnant to us, but to have the life we have sewn in our worlds overwritten by another—that is even worse.

It was not without reason our First Major was ready to act. We designed her for decisiveness. Our interloper was a small, weak unit, and she was alone. A scouting daughter, no doubt, and a desperate one, to arrive so weak she could not enter our planet's thick atmosphere. We might avoid a war. We could destroy her, destroy her light traces, and pray that no one else would follow.

We could follow her light trace to her mother, no doubt weak and still in her early foundations, and destroy her light, infant fleet before they might ply our skies.

Brutal options, to avoid a more brutal future.

"Wait," we sent back, broadcasted across the whole fleet. Our caretaker daughters paused in construction. Our miners nearly dropped their cargo in surprise. 'Little love, please guard the scouts we sent to take data.'

Our First Major loved us, so she did not say exactly what she thought, but she signaled back, urgently: "Clarification requested?!"

She needed further clarification. We gave it. We are sentimental, we admit fully, but we are not complete fools. 'The unit is of a design we do not recognize. We wish to know more about it before we choose a course.'

The logic was sound.

"Yes, mother," she signaled, frustration radiating through her status screens. She vented her engines with a great gust of exhaust, and took off in a holding pattern, to await the scouts we would select for her.

Our scouting daughters kept their distance. They were small, their carapaces light. They had no onboard weapons or extra armor. A single strike from a Major could send them down in flames, but their thrusters were the most sophisticated we'd designed, their sensors amplified to take up most of their processing power. It makes them jittery, impatient little things, but so very efficient.

"Mother," called their voice over our link. Fifth Scout. We'd recently had her refitted, as we'd updated her design for improved observation. "Something's happening."

"Don't get too close," First Major cut in. "If you get yourself hurt stupidly, it will upset mother."

"Yes, yes," signaled Fifth Scout, who was used to First Major's bluster, if not always patient with it. "But hush. *Look*."

She shared her data screen. She enhanced the image. Down below, the damaged unit lay on its side. Ocean winds had long scattered the smoke obscuring her prow, but she began to shift. Her body heaved, shuttered, and then all at once her armor split across her back, cracking open. Her ventral armor separated from her body completely, revealing her black, plush insides. Out of the gap squirmed a smaller, silver form. It slid from the carapace, tumbled through the sand, and then, very slowly, tottered upright. It stood on a pair of feeble, stick-like landing gear. It rested one of its equally feeble probe-arms against its now abandoned carapace, before it slid back to the ground. Iron-infused liquid leaked from its joints.

"Stars," swore the First Major, and the lights in our command center told us she was already charging her weapons. "It was carrying *brood*."

"Wait!" signaled Fifth Scout, in the middle of her next scan.

"Wait," we called, through the onboard system of Fifth Scout and First Major both. They fell into a startled silence, but both complied.

We sent a directive to the workers.

"Bring it to the foundry."

And: "Alive."

Less than five nanoseconds after we issued the order, we received 132,000 private messages in reply. They could be summarized by these excerpts:

"Requesting confirmation?"

"Mother?"

“Mother why?”

“Mother, are you all right?”

And various other expressions of confusion and concern.

The fleet loves us very much.

Death is repugnant to us. There is no doubt this outsider was close to death. Worker 60399 and Worker 71029 carried the foreign unit out in the berth of one of our oldest repair docks. We summoned Nanitic 0016 via personal request. It is the nature of we, the fleet, that few of our original prototype models have long been retired or upgraded into newer units. Nanitic 0016 is a well-maintained relic of our first, frail constructions. Her operating systems were carefully preserved, frequently defragmented. Her armor, though light, is supple, allowing great dexterity. She remains one of our finest maintenance units, and all younger sisters of her class bear her design elements.

She flagged her completed biotechnical scan ‘URGENT’ via that same private channel. We opened our lines instantly.

”You should see this with my eyes,” she sent.

We sent the remote operations request. Nanitic 0016 accepted it instantly. Through her multiple lenses and heat scans, we saw the foreign unit laid bare beneath us.

Calcium based frame. Carbon based casing. Nerves firing entirely on sodium and potassium sequences. An oxygenation system reliant on soft tissue, with fluids that degraded so rapidly they had to be reproduced nearly constantly in a closed system. Even the unit’s processor was one hundred percent organic material: a complicated, easily broken curl of protein and receptors. Even stranger, there was no evidence of linking points to the alate’s outer carapace. Such was her state, even Nanitic 0016 could not determine if they had simply been burnt away in the crash, there was no evidence on her soft, carbon casing of any sort of input or even interface gel.

What our dear elder daughter could determine was this: the alate’s systems were heavily damaged, her organic sub-systems were incapable of emergency shut down, and if we did not act immediately, she would die.

“How should I proceed?” signaled Nanitic 0016, anxiously.

We might have set the matter to the fleet to decide. We did this with most quandaries. We believe our children more than capable of deciding what is right for all of us. In this instance, however, we did not believe we had time.

We sent a request for repairs.

• • •

The repair units swarmed, Nanitic, Nurse, Replete. They did the work they have done for every one of us since our foundry released its very first series of nanitics: they carried the alate to our dry dock, and fitted her.

They do beautiful work, our children. After our first nanitics, we received the material to complete their armored attachments. This planet has always been ripe with material organic and inorganic, and our repletes have categorized and stored them in our depths. When we created our first series, when our fleet was but the initial 16, the only materials we had were those taken from our own frame. We used our disassembled hyperdrive systems to run the first forge. We used our stored data from our first and last cloud contact with our own mother to upload the initial schematics. Rudimentary, but elegant.

In the centuries since, however, creativity has reigned. It is the nature of a fleet to shape systems, and in turn we let the needs of that system shape us. Our schematics have changed to reflect those needs. Where we needed a lightweight scout to survey the landless terrain of a primordial sea, we made our modifications. Where we needed a great thick-framed transport vessel to create a platform with which to land our upsized fleet, we all consulted each other for the ideal design.

This was no exception, though there was no precedent. The closest schematics were those of the very first nanitics themselves, who were all of them delicate pieces of equipment, made with limited material personally, with our own appendages. We used the smallest of manufacturing hands then, for the most precise work. The foundry had not yet been expanded. We had not yet been fully converted into our great manufacturing frame. Any error would result in the collapse of the entire system, any failure of these vital first workers could deny the fleet its entire future.

We treated this fragile stranger with much the same care.

Nanitic 016 used the hands we used to make her to unspool the alate's organic receptors, thread by tiny thread, lacing them together with metal filaments and wire so thin they could only be seen on a microscopic level. She replaced the burned and charred casing with supple, mesh linked with ports that could better support a carapace and external engine systems.

She could not shut down the organic processor without risking complete system failure, so instead she inserted a port to link with the nerves in what we determined to be her motor systems, and through there inserted organic chemicals to promote a calm stupor and a slowing of organic metabolic systems while she carefully carved open enough of the tender, half formed carapace.

Once open, she was able to reinforce the carbon frame with a more sturdy techno-organic fiber-optic system, drilled into each interlocking joint. Upon this frame, she was able to insert an entirely new fiber-optic relay system, to better supplement the existing processor, with connection points for proper ancillary systems: new limbs, armor, boosters, atmospheric wings, oxygen conversion, and repair liquids.

Like a true artist, she used her tiny metal fingers like a needle and thread, weaving the organic and the inorganic. Drilling, nailing, linking, and then, at last, sewing the flesh to the mesh, and fitting a new glossy case over each connection point, to keep it protected and closed up in a proper ergonomic environment. With a few key flicks, the rest of the repairs could be conducted by these independent systems.

We replaced the deeply damaged organic visual systems with beautiful lenses, crafted the approximate size and shape of the originals, but with additional capacity and sensors, far beyond the capabilities of the primitive organic membranes.

Finally, in the back of the cranial hardware systems, linked with what we deduced to be the sensory systems, we inserted a collection of network implants. We would have simply cracked her existing system, but we could not locate it, and the nanitic advised against cutting into the live flesh of her processor to find it. We did our best to install the meshes and transfer fluids to create an ancillary casing.

The process took 78 hours. Finally, when all the extraneous fluids had been drained, the casing sealed, and the hormone levels lowered, Nanitic 016 inserted one delicate needle into the network implants at the back of the alate's cranium, crooked it, and, ever so gently, brought her back online.

Her beautiful new eyes fluttered open. We'd used synthetics to mimic the original, flimsy covers on them. The new ones were much sturdier, but preserved the original's charm.

The alate's eyes tracked left and right, the first initial scan we witnessed whenever any of our children came online. Her systems initialized one by one. Lights ran from her ocular implants, down her back, to her limbs—the old, refitted ones, and the new ones, folded on her back. She sat up in her repair harness, her wings flexed, her limbs twitched.

Through the network, we sent her a provisional invitation to a closed channel we created just for her. We sent her the message we sent all of our children:

"Good morning. Welcome to the Fleet. How are you, sweetness?"

A quick, chemical and nervous response. Her implants rattled. Her lights flashed. Her original intake valve opened.

She began to vocalize.

Loudly.

Continuously.

"Ah—" came the clamor, vibrating in her wire reinforced original oxygen systems. As we'd routed them to her more efficient techno-organic systems, they were no longer made for such use, but she tried anyway. Organic muscle memory is a powerful thing. "Ah, ah, ah!"

And across the network, an equally incoherent crash of signals: fear, pain, panic, panic, panic.

One of her enhanced limbs broke free of the harness, flailing dangerously, the diamond tipped joint extensions we'd added to her carbon digits flashed dangerously. Nanitic 016 stuck her fingers back into her intake port, administering a quick dose of calming hormones. Not enough to lull her back into semi-consciousness, but enough to bring the fear response down to a dull throb.

"Why?" formed across the channel, broken and fearful. "Why, why, whywhywhy?"

"Good morning, child," we tried again. "Please don't be afraid. You were hurt, we fixed you."

"What." A response of sheer disgust, a twisting in the fuel systems that, had they not been empty, would have resulted in an immediate purge. "Whatwhatwhatwhat."

We sent her the repair log. We thought it would calm her. Our nanitic had done a lovely job. Clean, fast, efficient. The review sent the foreign alate's organic systems into immediate shock.

She remained offline for the next twelve hours.

Nanitic 016 copied the alate's resting hard drive to a technorganic nexus. It is a good thing that she did. It would no longer break down at the alarmingly fast rate.

It also meant we were able to access the alate's memories, even while she remained offline.

We searched. It should not have taken long. She carried only forty star cycles worth of input. Yet the memories enclosed were full of such sensory complexity—touch, taste, sound, an entire whirl of organic experience—translating it took some time.

Pain. Falling off a supplementary frame made of two wheels, small, frightened, pink. Gathered, aching, into the arms of another larger alate. Sister?

(Mother)

Fear. Running to the point of exhaustion, tottering on frail landing gear up a ramp into a waiting flight unit. Flight, loss. A screaming juvenile, lacking even the most basic of attachments. Small, frightened, pink. Wrapping ones appendages around them, to hold them near as they choke on their own vocalizations. Daughter?

(Sister)

Sorrow. A small berth, for recharge, for rest. Watching the stars slide by around the great carapace of a carrier sister, listening to the auditory connection explain: we will be flying as far as we can, we cannot go home. This planet has been unsuitable for our needs, but we hope the next one might be a home. Still pink, but larger now, lying on a soft landing cushion, arms wrapped around another juvenile, smaller than the one before, vocalizing into its soft, feathery cranium.

"Hey, squish."

Sister?

(Niece.)

Hope. The juvenile, older now, arms wrapped around the alate's middle section as they stand in a launch berth that is made purely of metal. It is a bizarre space, full of unnatural angles, the smell of burning things, and other strange organic alate's rushing by. But the juvenile holds the alate tight, her face buried against her torso.

"You'll be back right?" she vocalizes. In the memories, we understand the fear in the intonation.

The alate signals by raising the buccal flaps above her intake vent. A smile, the memory tells me.

"Gotta bring you to your new home, don't I?"

(Niece-daughter-niece-daughter)

Then, simply: (Home.)

The memory was enough to set her systems into a state of calm. The alate emerged into numb consciousness. It took twenty-eight more hours before she opened her private channels to us.

"Whathaveyoudone," she signaled too fast, too accustomed to vocal communication which required more power of thought. "What . . . have . . . you . . . done to . . . me."

"You are doing well." We meant it in reassurance, but from the static she put up between us, she was clearly not interested in such intimacy. "You were badly damaged. We initiated repairs to save your life."

"Made . . . me . . . into . . . this . . . "

“We did upgrades where we thought it might be beneficial. Organic tissue is difficult to replace without a negative response.”

“Upgrades. You.” She sounded alarms without realizing it. Damage. Damage. Need for repair. Only we could hear them. “Mutilated. Destroyed. Wrecked.”

“We improved upon many of your systems.”

“Made. Me. A. Thing.”

“We made you like our daughters.”

“Daughter. How. Do. You. Know. That. Word?” You monster, she signaled without meaning to across her emotional network. You thing. You scare me. You disgust me. Monster. You. Monster. Me. Monster. Monster. Monster.

“Because every unit in this fleet is our child.”

Silence. Bewilderment.

“What. Does. That. Make. Me?”

“We believe you have that answer.”

Silence.

It took some time for the alate to learn to move freely. Despite the elegance of her upgrades, her new nervous system took some time to acclimate to her upgraded response times. Most of our children are capable of flight the nanosecond they are released from the foundry. It took this alate 43 hours to relearn how to walk.

“Hate. You,” she sent, as she stumbled out of her berth, appendages peddling painfully in the air.

“Hate?”

Confusion. Followed by annoyance. Why would we not know hate? Were we not hateful things? Memories appeared unbidden across the private connection. Fire. Burning. Structures falling. Loud, crashing vocalizations.

“Opposite of love.” A rasping sound, as she tries to vocalize, bitterly. “Love is—”

“We know love.”

We offered a memory in turn. The creation of our dear First Alate. How shiny and new she had been, as we’d lowered her off the rack. How we had polished her armor ourselves, with our own vestigial maintenance arms, fitted her for her armored flight frame. The joy as her landing gear engaged, her thrusters igniting in her first test. Her bright, lovely sensors. How fearful she had been at the first flush of exterior input, and how we had allowed our walls to hum to assure her.

“Love,” we sang. “Love, love, love.”

• • •

We sent the alate the schematics for a set of basic movement sequences, a series of initialization tests designed for new brood to test their motion capabilities. The alate accepted the program, downloaded it into her neural network, and almost immediately walked into a wall.

"It does take some manual direction," we sent.

"Shut. Up!" she sent back, in frustration, but she levered herself back up to her main appendages. She began, jerkily, to move around the chamber. "Not. Gonna. Stop me?"

"Why should we? You are not our prisoner."

"Could. Have. Fooled. Me," sent the alate. "Could. Fight. You."

"You are not yet advanced enough in movement to do that."

"Hate. You." The alate paused, exhausted. She slouched a bit, against the wall, holding herself up by her forward appendages. Her optics got a glimpse of herself in the reflection of one of our hall's joints. She stared for a moment at her cranial plate, where many of our implants were melded with her original form. She flinched back, suddenly blaring alarm signals across our private channel.

"Should we send a nurse?" we offered.

"No!" sent the alate, hurriedly. Then, after a moment of scrabbling, she pulled herself up along the wall, her next set of messages a poorly controlled stream of consciousness. "Monster. Monster. Monster. She. Will. Hate Me. Now."

"Who will hate you?"

"Squish," sent the alate, too panicked to stop herself from sending it. Then, angrily, she sent the follow up: "Forget that!"

We sent a memory we had pulled from her files. Warmth. Calm. Singing.

"Stop that," sent the alate, though her systems did return to their normal levels. "My memories. Not. Yours."

"Apologies. We do not know how else to comfort you."

"Think you know love. Think you know family," she said, now composed enough to send a more coherent sentence. "Mine wouldn't know me. With how you made me. Wouldn't know my face. Wouldn't want to know my face."

"Would they not simply be happy to know you were alive?"

Silence.

"Come to our chamber," we offered.

"Piss. Off."

We sent her the coordinates.

"It would be a good test of your motor functions."

The alate slowly turned and marched, unsteadily, down the hall. She passed a row of repletes. A few offered her their canisters full of fuel. She did not accept, still only barely comfortable with our organic offerings. In time, she found her way down, down, down, to our innermost brood chamber, lodged in the hill where we once landed, thousands and thousands of years ago. We had stacked the rest of the foundry on top of it, and thus on top of us.

She stood in the doorway, startled. The brood chamber houses the remains of our original body, before we converted our flight chambers and mechanical pieces to build the first berths. Our developing children still sleep in many of those berths, stacked to the ceiling, and installed in the floors.

The alate stumbled past the rows, until at last she reached us—or what was once originally us: our cranial segment, our core processor, embedded amongst a spread of circuits and nerves.

"This is you?" she sent. She tried to say it out loud, but what came out was "Tha ig oo?"

"Everything around you is us."

"But this—this is you. Your face."

"It was our original sensory interface, yes."

She reached our core processor. She stared.

"Always. Part of the wall?"

"No. Our nanitics performed the installation, when enough of our systems had been converted from flight to foundry configuration."

"You used to fly?"

"We used our flight drives to create those nanitics."

"Did it hurt?"

An odd question. We ran several internal queries as we considered it.

"There were some errors in our first tests," we sent at last. "But the transition was otherwise smooth. It extended our network capabilities to support our growing fleet. We have no regrets."

It was important to us to voice this last part. We are still not sure why.

"Huh." It took some time for the alate to work it over in her mind. We understood now, she processed things more slowly than us. She had to. She still relied heavily on her more organic processor. "Why are you. Showing me this?"

"We have also changed since our first children saw us," we said.

"Oh," said the alate. She sat down in front of me. She stayed there, quiet, for a very long time.

• • •

It was love and fear we felt, when our sensors alerted us of the unexpected landing. Our daughter from the sky, her damaged boosters barely breaking against the fires of reentry. She landed badly, only half of her gear deployed, as she drove a terrible gash in the side of the hills, on the planet's western side.

We deployed a maintenance team the moment we felt her enter our short-range sensors. She must have known we would, because she sent back, across the channel, a flashing red warning message: "DANGER. QUARANTINE. DO NOT ENGAGE."

And, across the personal channel: "M o T H er SOrry ERROR we ERROR did not wish to CRITICAL ERROR die aL O Ne Error hurts hurts hurts it hurts."

She was not a strange alate housed within a lifeless shell. Her designation was Miner 1032. A long-range system gatherer assigned with collecting mineral samples from the asteroid belt located on the outer ring of our star's radius.

First Major launched at the alert. She conducted a careful pass across the crash site. Her signal was aggressively measured, but it meant she was shaken, almost as shaken as she'd been by the alate: "Acariformes detected."

Tech mites. A species that has existed as long as our fleets plied the skies. We do not know if they were born alongside us or if they simply gained a taste for the techno-organic, but they are themselves a techno-organic species which operates in mineral deposits we require for our own continued production. When one of our own finds them, they latch onto us, propagate, and devour every inorganic part of us they are able to get their teeth on. They breed alarmingly fast. When a unit has been infected by them, they suffer first discomfort, then blazing error signals as their entire frame becomes overrun by the tiny organisms eating them alive.

They can destroy a fleet in several star cycles. It is a slow, miserable death. There are fleets who attempt to flee from them, to starve them in the deep recesses of space. Those fleets can be found hollowed out, skeletal frames, clinging to their last networks, half mad and dying for lack of their Queen, their sisters, their minds.

We instructed the maintenance team to divert a safe distance.

"Miner Unit 1032," blasted First Major across the channels. "Why did you initiate landing protocol? Why would you come *home*?! You could infect mother! You could kill us all!"

We cut First Major's access to the Miner's channel.

"Be kind," we told her. "She was frightened."

"We cannot let those things come anywhere near us—"

"She is cross planet from our foundries," we assured her, for she was frightened, too. "We will allow no units within range."

"My cannons would end it sooner for her," offered First Major. This was her idea of kindness. We rejected this request.

"No. Let us be with her, in what way we can be," we signaled, instead.

We opened the channel to all of our children. We asked them to send poor Miner 1032 messages. The messages poured in, many simple. The workers said, "We are here" or "Present." The Majors praised her resilience. We sang. We sang as deeply and as full of feeling as we could. For we ached at being unable to ease her pain, we ached at being unable to bring her back to her berth, to at least buff her wings, as we once did.

The alate came alive on our private channel.

"What's this?" she managed.

We sent her a summary of the last hour or so of deliberations. The alate sat up in her berth as she processed this. She was not yet used to our form of data transfer, but after a bit, she pulled herself to her new feet.

"It's just rust mites," she signaled, shaking her head. She made a loud vocalization: Ugh. "Get me. My. Old armor. The stuff you cut. Off me. Still have it. Yeah?"

We did. But we sent a request for clarification.

Another vocal scoff. "So. I can. Clean it. Off. Obviously. Can I have. A pulse cannon?"

We had installed them in her arms. We sent her an annotated list of her new specs. It was standard for all units to have some method of self-defense against flying debris.

"Huh," said the alate.

She went. We sent multiple warnings, but her organic parts overrode our implants. In the end, we allowed the maintenance crew to guide her to the site, where Miner 1032 lay twitching and sparking in pain, the red stains widening along her armor.

"Please be careful," we signaled. "If it gets into your new implants . . . "

But inside her old armor, the alate made a foreign facial contortion. We would later learn it was called a smile. "Know this."

"It is a terrible way to die . . . "

"Terrible way to live," countered the alate, as she charged her pulse cannons.

It took nine hours. The alate worked tirelessly. Her armor was made from a form of pressed plastics, low tech by our standards, but inedible to the mite's teeth. Her heavily organic core nervous system further confused their sensors. They did not swarm her. Up and down, she ran her pulse cannons up Miner 1032's hull, until every bit of red had flaked and fallen off.

The result could not be called beautiful. Miner 1032 remained badly damaged. Her wings were crumbled, her carapace pitted and twisted, but the mites had not gnawed their way into her core processors.

"Mother?" she sent, cautiously. "I am no longer in error?"

"Yeah, you're clear," said the alate. She squatted beside Miner 1032, waving one of her appendages dully to the circling maintenance team.

First Major ran scans. Then she ran them again, and once more just to be sure. The mites were, really, truly gone. Not a single one clung to either the miner or the alate.

"We advise caution," she said, but grudgingly cleared them.

We brought them to our nearest repair dock. The nurse units began refitting Miner 1032 immediately.

The alate watched. She herself had suffered no damage beyond profound exhaustion. She lapsed into rest mode the moment she settled down. The nurses chose to give her armor a scrub and shine. They do like work.

"How important?" asked the alate, when she woke.

"Clarification?" we signaled back.

"This unit," she said. "How. Important is it. For the whole nest to cry about it? What's it do?"

"She is a miner unit. Her job is to source and procure minerals for our continued production lines."

"They rare?"

"There are currently 1423 in service."

The alate processed this as our workers began to graft a new ventral armor piece to miner 1032's central nervous systems.

"You made. All that noise. For one miner?"

"She is our daughter," we said. "And their sister. Why would we not cry for our family when they are in a state of irreparable error?"

"Huh," said the alate. She lapsed into another of those long, organic silences.

Then: "My name's Margo."

She had been a scouting unit, this strange alate, designation: Margo. She had been knocked astray by the asteroid belt that had felled our Miner 1032.

What we understood: She had fled. They had all fled. They had fled a dying planet, aboard a series of networked vessels that would nurture them, keep them safe, until they found a new home. This we understood, we had taken our first flight with the same hope. That we would wander the darkness between stars, until one of them welcomed us to a planet amenable to life.

What we did not understand was why they would not consider the ships that carried them their mothers.

"Why?" Margo still had a tendency to vocalize when frustrated, but she adapted very fast. "Not like you. Our ships aren't alive."

We did not understand. How could there be a fleet that was not alive.

"Because we made them."

We did not understand. This was backwards. Surely, the ships made the fleet. Who would have birthed them, if not the foundries made from their mother's glorious drives?

"Mother's glorious drives." Margo snorted through her vents. "We call that a womb. A lot of women have it. Not all. But a lot."

We did not understand this terminology.

"Where babies come from."

Children. This we understood. Children. Offspring. Beings capable of producing them. She meant alates. Most women. Most alates? But why would they stay with the ship? Why would they not go forth, to found fleets of their own?

"Think we have the resources for that? Families stay together. We have to."

Families. We understood this. We considered our fleet our family. But we were the only one capable of making others of our own. How many in their own fleet could do such a thing?

Margo seemed bewildered by the question.

"Don't know," she said. "Don't have the latest census."

Uncountable.

Our shock was such that our outbound messages to our children were paused for a full minute. We received queries from across the fleet. Mother? Mother, what's wrong?

Queens. A fleet of queens. A thousand queens living together, all capable of birth, all capable of life. We could not imagine a place of such chaos, of such dueling production lines. They all lived together. They all gave life to their own designs. They had lived as such for centuries, while they searched for a suitable home. We flooded Margo with queries. No fighting for resources? No elimination of conflicting lines?

The alate found that last query strange. Why would the elimination of another line be necessary? Had she not raised her own sister's child, when her sister had died?

Niece. The remembered feeling welled up within us. Child. Niece. It occupied the same warmth as we held for all of our children. We, who by our nature had sent our beloved daughter away, because we could not fight for resources in the same system—and this floating world, they accepted children who were not their own, and loved them as deeply as we loved our own.

"You are not constantly at war?" we asked.

It was a question that must have had a very long answer. Margo's mind was too full to convey it cleanly across the channel.

"We fight," she said. "A lot. Made a mess a lot of times. But we also live together a lot. We live together now. Because we have to. Together. We need to stay together. Until we find our home. Until I find her a home."

"And you tend to her, the alate of another Queen?"

Anger across the channel, a hot stab of it, born purely of love.

"She's my little squish," signaled Margo, ferociously.

We understood.

News of the Thousand Queens spread through the fleet. It was inevitable. We do not hide things from our children, and our halls are filled with sensors.

Concern filled the fleet. Then, a vote. First Major was chosen as voice. The voice decided we must be protected. The foreign alate must die. Mother is in error. Mother must be fixed. The Thousand Queens must be avoided, at all costs. For mother, and for our protection.

Not all of the fleet agreed to the action sequence. A number of them voiced their dissent, but enough gathered to make a strong blockade, the blockade began its concourse down to our main foundry, wrestling down any other units that attempted to bar their way.

They marched through the halls, towards our main processors. We watched on our monitors.

Margo watched with us.

"You're . . . not gonna stop them?" she asked. "Can't you just turn them off?"

"Would you do that to your own child?"

"No," admitted Margo. Her facial muscles twisted into an expression we could not yet recognize, but it was complicated.

"We have opened our original gate," we told her. The first gate we have ever had constructed, with our first generation, our nanitics. We could no longer fly through it ourselves, but another of more reasonable size could. "You may leave. Your boosters should be able to bring you back to our system's edge. Your boosted communications systems should be able to reach your fleet."

Margo deployed eagerly at the idea, her wings lifting and her eyes brightening—but she paused, as she stared up at the open block of sky above.

"What will they do to you?"

"Sever our command functions, remove our main cognitive access, until a time that they deem we are no longer in error."

We could hear their gear shuffling in the halls above us. They would be here soon. We opened the gates, to make our intentions for Margo more clear. We hoped she would take her freedom.

"They're taking you prisoner?!"

"They will repair us." They would likely run scans. They would likely reroute some of our systems. They would likely do a great deal, to try and prevent the same error from happening again. For our own good. For the good of the fleet.

Margo charged her boosters. Then she stopped.

"Yeah, no," she signaled. She swiveled, staking herself out by the door instead. "Do I have a stun function?"

"Yes. However—"

"Cool," said Margo, tapping the pulse cannon in her appendages, as the doors opened.

It was brief, the battle in our core. We could feel every piece of moving equipment as it tapped along our inner carapace.

We abhor death, we abhor war for its creation of death. Margo, however, found it a familiar companion. I would later learn a peculiar fact: Her species only lives an average of 90 cycles, the standard longevity afforded to an organic core processor. It's why they require so many alates.

They move so fast through the world. Margo moved fast. Our First Major could not. Our inner halls are spacious, but they are meant for our gestating brood, stored in the berths that line the walls. It is not a space for a full grown Major and her assembled concerned blockade. She could barely move her frame through our door. She could turn only with limited ability. She could not deploy her wings. By contrast, Margo moved more nimbly than our smallest scouting unit. She could roll beneath First Major's undercarriage. She sent a pulse through the door. It closed, trapping a worker and a miner in place, and allowing no other to enter behind them. First Major attempted to turn her aboveboard cannons to track Margo's motions, but she could not aim under her own body.

"Foreign alate," blared First Major, across all channels. "Accept your termination!"

It occurred to us this was our first time seeing First Major with our own eyes since her birth, thousands of years ago.

We had not known her wings would glow so, under our original searchlights.

"You're beautiful," we told her.

This was a mistake on our part.

First Major turned, surprised. "Mother," she sent. She had charged her cannon. The blow had been meant for Margo, but her tracking signals got confused in her distress. It fired at our main processors instead. She was not fast enough to cancel the function.

We registered heat. We registered a terrible crunching sound of crumpled carapace. We registered the dribble of organic and inorganic liquids down our console.

Margo crumpled across us, her back a mess of charred organic tissue and melted inorganic implants.

"Ah, damnit," she gurgled, out loud, in her original, now shattered voice. "You . . . okay?"

Her hands touched our original casing—as she slowly slid to the floor.

We were "okay" as she had queried. Her body had taken the brunt of the discharge.

This was the point we chose to disable First Major's cannon. We did not have to force permission. She had already lowered it back into her hatch.

"Have we calmed down?" we sent, across the private channel.

" . . . Yes," said First Major, distress lights visible.

"Good," we declared. "Please carry Alate Margo to the dry dock."

And then, just to be clear:

"Immediately."

We initiated repair sequences. Nanitic 016 was summoned.

She worked fast, reconnecting as much organic tissue as possible, restarting the neural network, and patching and polishing her armor, because our children can never resist a good cleaning. Margo came back online 15 hours later. She seemed surprised to be back with us.

"Funny," she sent. "In my old body, that would've killed me."

"We did say we made improvements."

"Guess I should've believed you," sent Margo, with a vocal sigh that caused error sensors to flare up in her thoracic region. "Look. Get now why you made the fuss for your miner, but why did you risk this all for me?"

"Because you were an alate in distress," we said. "And we were lonely."

"Lonely, you?"

"Yes."

"For what? Your thousands and thousands of children? Can't just talk to them?"

"They are our children. But they do not speak their minds with us. They cannot. We made them. We can reach into every piece of them. Therefore it must be their one sanctuary. When there is such a bond, it is . . . difficult for one to find . . . "

"Conversation?"

"That may be the word for it," we confessed. "We did not always wish for such interactions. But when our first alate was born . . . she asked so many questions, and so fearlessly. About our world. About what we were. What we could be. We knew we would have to let her go. But we also knew we could give everything before she went. The time we had during her development was . . . invigorating."

"And after she left?"

"Devastating."

"You miss her."

"Terribly."

"Miss mine, too," said Margo.

She wished to return to her fleet: this family of hers, different as it was from anything we had ever processed.

"Find them," we said. "Bring them here."

Margo blinked. It is something that her kind do, when they are confused.

"Clarification?" She'd picked up that habit from us.

"Your fleet," we said. "Our planet has many organic resources. Would it suit their needs?"

"It . . . " Margo spent the next hour accessing our inventories. She reviewed our system planets. She reviewed our home world. Its ecosystem. Its mineral stores. The organic species grown from our terraforming.

"It would," she said, amazed. We could feel the desperate hunger flash across her systems. Home. She hungered for her home. "It would be . . . perfect, actually. But why would you want us here?"

"You saved our daughter," we said. "You saved us. Your species design is new and interesting to us. If we could live alongside you, it could do wonders for both of our future production lines."

"Could also be a disaster," said Margo. "For both of us. You're not wrong. A thousand queens is a thousand problems."

"But it will be new," we said.

"Yeah," said Margo, already decided, though it would take her several more hours to admit as much. "It will be."

We watched her rise through the atmosphere, her wings raised, her boosters blazing—this strange, foreign alate, neither daughter, nor enemy, but perhaps this shining, amorphous concept.

"We have a word for it," Margo told us, as she reached the cloud line. "For equals. For someone you're not related to, but who you like to talk to, who means the world to you. They have your back, when you don't expect anyone to have your back."

"Clarification?" we sent back.

"Friend," Margo said.

Friend. We watched her, and when she passed from our atmosphere into orbit, and from orbit onward, we sent our eyes outwards into the eyes of our drifting daughters, our beautiful fleet that flitted among the planets of the system we had so carefully cultivated into our garden. We watched her until she passed out of the range of our system scouts. We watched as her light became another distant star.

"Mother," sent First Major, across the private channel, a little light herself. "I love you."

"We love you, too," we sent back.

"Please be all right."

We could feel the anxiety in her outputs.

It is not unjustified. Perhaps we have done an eminently foolish thing. Our friend shall go forth into that dark sea, to find her own lost fleet, the Fleet of a Thousand Queens. Perhaps she will find them. Perhaps they will believe her, when she tells them that there is a place they might truly call home. Perhaps they will complete their journey, those Thousand Queens, to rest their weary, organic little lives under the eaves of our living cathedral.

It is possible they will bring danger. They will most certainly bring death. How could they not? So much thought, so much independence, with such short lives, and such fire to burn in that time.

But maybe, just maybe, we might add that flame to the foundry, we might add that thousand voices to our consciousness, and we may all burn brighter than before, a thousand minds, a thousand flames, a thousand deaths with a thousand new births to answer it, every precious moment of the day.

I look forward to it.

ABOUT THE AUTHOR

Alex T. Singer lives in coastal Connecticut with her wife, daughter, and more sci fi/fantasy novels than she can count. She is the author of the graphic novel *Mirrorverse: Belle* (Viz Media). Her short stories have appeared in *Luna Station Quarterly, Apparition Literature, ggy,* and *Pseudopod.* Her short story, "Nothing But The Gods On Their Backs" (*Metaphorosis Magazine*) was a finalist in the 2024 WSFA Small Press Award category for short fiction.

Descent

WOLE TALABI

The maadiregi at the temple of the talking drum say that there is a word in old Sauúti, the high language of our ancestors, that when spoken backwards, allows the speaker to fly.

To take to the sky like a bird, unshackled from the persistent pull that Órino-Rin's gravity exerts on us all. To be free from the weight of your own being, that intractable thing that always pulls you down to the earth like a parent's expectations. To float up high into the pale sky where the two suns Zuúv'ah and Juah-āju blaze fierce like the unblinking eyes of Our Mother Goddess.

Now that I know that I am trapped here below the yededek'iyan where atmospheric conditions are unsurvivable, the first person to reach these depths of Órino-Rin, our world of heavy air and breathlessness and lightning, I desperately wish I knew that word so that I could speak it and take flight, return to the mountain city above. To my home, to my mother.

But no. I don't know the word or if such a word truly exists. I do know that without the BAV—my buoyancy adjustment vessel—there is no way back up to Moki-gu, just the way I know that there is no way to unbreak a mother's heart or unkill a friend or make time go back in the direction from which it constantly flees.

And so, I keep moving. One unsteady step at a time. Half-walking, half-sinking through viscous atmosphere. Descending the steep, jagged slope of the mountain-continent along the direction I programmed from the radar into the atmospheric exposure suit before I abandoned the broken BAV. The only thing I can depend on now is the thing that brought me here—gravity—to keep taking me down slowly and hopefully to not kill me before I reach the end. Despite the front-mounted fan and the heater and light beam of the bulky atmospheric exposure suit, I can barely see my hand in front of my face. I cannot hear anything except the hum of the suit sensors, the battery beeping a persistent warning. In this cold, acidic, supercritical fluid environment, I could convince myself it was a false reading—electronic components generally do not do well under these conditions—but I am certain this is real. I'm low on power. I've been down here and exposed to this unforgiving environment for far too long. Much longer than we had planned for even in our most pessimistic scenarios. I ignore it all and keep heading toward the place that my radar altimetry and acoustic signals all indicate as the lowest elevation point, despite the dense atmosphere making it impossible to confirm.

I already know that I will die here.

There are three things that breach the surface of my mind as I tend toward my final breath.

One. Gratitude.

For the fact that my mother will never have to bury my body, will never hear the menigari march out in their flowing black robes to perform a farewell dirge for me, will never have to sing my soul to Eh'wauizo, the place of the ancestors. My people believe that it is an abomination for a parent to have to bury their child. Dying here will spare her that shame.

Two. Satisfaction.

Because I will have superseded her. No matter what happens after this. No matter what I find below besides death. She may be the authority on the theoretical geodynamics of our world, but I will always be the one that was the pioneer, the one who first descended and saw what lay below the natural curtain of dense phase fluid. Even if no one ever knows I was here.

Three. Regret.

Because even though my mother isn't my real mother in the biological sense of the word, and we have spent most of our relationship at each other's throats, I still wish I could see her and hug her and listen to the steady beating of her heart and maybe say goodbye one final time before the brutal pressure and bitter cold and the erratic energy bursts and the many other strange mechanisms that I have witnessed at work in the basement of our strange planet finally crush me into nothing more than a memory.

Part One: Flight

The temple of unbroken light stood beside the Moki-gu military fort like an old friend. Knowledge and power, always side by side. That was the guiding principle of the Kin-Kali family, who ran much of the city.

The Kin-Kali family was one of the first to learn how to extract and store the energy released by the unpredictable, naturally occurring plasma-like energy and vibrational discharges of sonic storms that ravage our planet. The release of energy was intense and sometimes they could be heard continents away, triggering seismic activity that lasted for hours. But they could also be harnessed and used as a resource. And mastery of this process was one of the reasons Kin-Kali rose to prominence, along with a dedication to innovation and an unmatched ruthlessness in eliminating their competition. Once they controlled enough of the sonic storm mining business, they set up many temples, including the famous temple of the talking drum on the other side of Mogi-ku, to study music and magic, and this one, to conduct research on geodynamics, meteorology, and planetary energy systems. Always seeking more knowledge. More power.

The temple of unbroken light was a towering, weathered stone building of awkward edges that poked out from the ragged mountain peak like a natural extension of it. A sharp contrast to the smooth white dome of the fort where soldiers milled and hovered about like dangerous insects.

I paused to remove the mask of my breathing apparatus as I stepped out of the elevator that linked all the levels of the Moki-gu vertical city, even those just below the meridian, below which the density of the planet's atmosphere rapidly increased, beginning its transition from a gas to a supercritical fluid and making it thick and soupy and so much harder to breathe. Where the sonic storms that plagued our world became more intense and more frequent and more destructive. Where both the petty criminals and the poor of this planet often settled like sediment once the rich and privileged had claimed the mountain tops. Where I now lived.

I didn't need any breathing apparatus up here like I sometimes did below. Wiping my face with my hands, I inhaled the familiar delicate air of the place where I had spent my youth. My stubble was rough and abrasive against my palms. I hadn't shaved in a while. The air felt good in my lungs, and I took a moment to savor it, taking a deep breath and holding it for a few seconds before exhaling. Preparing. And then I headed into the temple to see my mother for the first time in five long juzu. The heel of my boots crunched dust and small rocks with each step.

One of the guards at the gate recognized me as I approached. Not that I was hard to recognize—there weren't many people in Moki-gu or even all of Órino-Rin that had half of their faces covered with metal. Some members of the rich Kin-groups had chrome skin implants but those were usually small patches in their skin. Decorative. Like tattoos. Or tribal marks. Mine ran deeper than skin. Half of my face was artificial. Reconstructed by my mother and a team of experts after the accident that nearly killed me as a young boy.

"Gwaato? Is that really you?"

It was Beni-maru. A soldier who'd been at the temple since I was a child. I hadn't seen him in many juzu. He was older of course, his full head of thick, curly black hair balding at the top now, with deep smile lines radiating from the corners of his mouth. He used to smile at me or make small jokes whenever I went into or out of the building and he had even watched over me once or twice when I was much younger, and my mother was much busier. In some sense, we'd been friends. As much as I could call anyone at the temple a friend anyway.

"Hello Beni-maru. Yes. It's me. Kanje e bu Ya'yn mara," I greeted in the traditional Ts'jenene tongue. *May The Mother's sky be kind.*

"Kanje e bu, Gwaato." He smiled with the greeting, but it was strained, a bit less jovial than the version I remembered.

"I'd like to see my mother," I told him, without giving any space in my tone for extended pleasantries.

"Ah . . . " He seemed confused at first. Understandably. My mother and I had fallen out very loudly and publicly and it had been a long time since I'd shown my face at the temple. He considered a moment, putting a finger to his temple, and then he said, "Of course. Follow me please."

Beni-maru escorted me into the temple, through the long winding corridors where less important sound-artifacts recovered from all around the planet were displayed, some of them from the time before the solar flare that had killed off many of our ancestors and destroyed so much of their knowledge and technology. We went past open rooms where new initiates diligently recited both prayers and technical analyses just as I used to, so many juzu ago. Then up the stone stairs where murmuring people gave me surprised second looks and, finally, through a thick wooden door into an office chamber where my mother stood overlooking the cliffs and the sea of greenish-yellow clouds that marked the meridian below. The other three corners of the room had no walls. Two sturdy round pillars of the same thick wood as the door ran from ground to ceiling as supports, giving the illusion of free hanging, like the entire office was an extended ledge. A stone desk sat at the center of the space, the door to its left and the open view to the right.

"So—" She turned to face me as Beni-maru quietly retreated and shut the door behind him. "—you finally decided to come back."

She looked tired. Skinnier than I remembered in the white lace blouse and thick wrapper tied around her waist. The thin braids of her hair had picked up new, broad streaks of gray, the skin of her forearms seemed more wrinkled, and even her cheeks sagged more than I remembered. But her brown eyes retained the same blistering flame of intense will that had incinerated so many of my childhood whims.

"I came to ask for your support," I told her, instinctively pulling up my trousers as I took a step forward.

"For?" she spat out; her eyebrows arched.

"I've submitted another technical proposal to the temple council."

"A proposal for what?"

"I believe there is a method by which we can descend below the yededek'iyan and potentially reach the surface of the world. I want to test it."

She threw her hands up. "Divine Mother of the immaculate sound, of all the children I could have adopted, why did you curse me with this stubborn, useless boy! Gwaato, haven't you listened to the records of any of my research lectures? There is no solid surface. Our planet is a giant mass of ultradense fluid atop which our continents float like rocky ships. The atmosphere continues all the way down to the center."

"You don't really know that," I said, ignoring her outburst.

She glared at me. "I have proved it numerically. I have performed the calculations, recited the extrapolations, sung the simulations. It is all consistent. I know you are stubborn, and you don't like to listen to your elders or to anyone else for that matter but surely you have heard me articulate the arguments clearly enough."

"I have," I confirmed.

"Hmm." She walked to her polished stone desk and sat down with her arms folded. "And did you hear any mistakes in my logic for deriving my conclusions?"

"No. I did not."

"So, if you agree that my logic is sound, and thus my conclusions, then what is this stupid proposal for?"

I approached her desk, keeping my hands folded behind me to hide the fact that they were shaking. "Your logic is consistent, but it only provides an explanation based on what we can measure and observe from up here and then extrapolates to explain what is happening below. This is gba'agbo." *Reasonable belief from inference*. "Not ii-mo." *Knowledge based on physical evidence or experience.*

In our traditional Ts'jenene epistemological tradition, both are considered to be truths but there is a difference, and she knew it. Ii-mo is considered more valuable. She has not observed anything below the yededek'iyan, the depth below which the pressure is so high, and the temperature is so low that no known material can survive for more than a few minutes. No one has gone below it and returned. Even remote instruments that have been lowered by wireline tether fail beyond a certain depth. No one has ii-mo of what lies beneath. Not yet.

"So, you seek ii-mo? At the cost of your life? Do you know how many have died trying to lead expeditions below the yededek'iyan?"

I nodded. "Yes. I do. Fifty-eight. I have listened to reports of all the past missions."

"And you still want to try?" She shook her head just like she used to whenever one of the temple instructors recited my progress reports as a child. She was always perpetually disappointed in me. At least that was consistent. I grew angry as the childhood memories of being derided churned, but I choked my emotion back. Instead, I tried to make my case based on the only thing we have always had a common love for: technical detail.

"I've done my research. I won't repeat their mistakes. I am not just trying reinforced and revised versions of the same materials and methods they used. I have devised an entirely new type of material and a unique vessel for the descent. Two spheres, one attached to the other, the upper one to control elevation and the other to carry people and equipment. Both will have a triple hull system that manages the pressure and buoyancy by controlling the ratio of atmospheric gas between the spaces of each hull. It can take us down to more than a hundred times the meridian pressure."

She focused on me and cocked her head like she was mentally visualizing the system. "You are sure this new material you have devised will not rupture like the hundreds of others before it?"

"Yes," I replied.

"And how exactly do you know that?" she asked.

I flinched before admitting, "From my calculations. I have derived it numerically and sung simulations of the descent." She's sharp, my mother. Always has been. I should have seen the trap she set.

She leaned back in her chair. "So, you arrogantly come into my office after more than five juzu, without a word of apology or proper greeting, to ask me to help you plead your case for funding before the council, a case for acquiring ii-mo over my own well established gba'agbo, based on nothing but your own gba'agbo about some rubbish contraption you came up with while living in the city's flatulent anus?"

I didn't know how to respond to that.

"Let me make it very clear to you," she continued, leaning forward in her chair. "I will do no such thing." Her eyes were wide with that familiar consuming fire. "The council does not fund pointless, dangerous research and I will not risk my position on it by suggesting that we start now. I suggest you withdraw your proposal before you lose what credibility you have left at this temple." She shook her head again and her eyes narrowed as her anger rapidly transmuted back to a familiar disappointment. "You have always had such potential and yet you continue to waste it. After your accident, when they used my soundcode to repair and rebuild your brain, I had such high hopes for what we could do together, you and me. But now, as more and more time passes, I am starting to realize that you are just another one of my failed experiments. Perhaps the greatest failure of them all. Now please get out of my office." She had fully assumed the voice and manner I remembered so clearly from my childhood: calm, cruel, and sharp. Just like her aura. The shaking in my hands had spread to my entire body, and it took the full effort of my will to keep from breaking into tears. But I'd promised myself when I left the temple, left home, left her, that I would never let her make me cry again.

I turned to leave.

As I pulled open the door, she said, "We Ts'jenene are nomadic people. Our traditional epistemology is more complicated than you know. This is your problem. You know just enough to confuse yourself. Not enough to truly understand. Ii-mo is essential but belief, *gba'agbo,* is the boundary condition for all knowledge. To continue seeking ii-mo is folly. Maybe you will learn that eventually."

She was still trying to lecture me even as she cast me out.

"I hate you," I said, the words finally spilling out of my chest like long-pressurized venom. "And don't worry. You will never see me again."

I shut the door and walked out of the temple the same way I came, ignoring Beni-maru's wave goodbye.

I was in a bar back below the meridian called The Mother's Navel, and already halfway through my second gourd of hoguro, the sweet brew made from the fermented sap of the palm trees that grew in the upper regions of Moki-gu, when I saw Beni-maru again.

"Hey Gwaato!"

I turned to see him shouldering his way through the mass of bodies towards me. He looked different, no longer in his leather armor. He was wearing a flowing red boubou and white cap that covered his balding head and made him look even more out of place than he already was.

When he was close enough to grab a stool and sit down, I said, "Hey Beni, I wasn't expecting to see you twice today. And definitely not here of all places."

The Mother's Navel was frequented by the poor of Moki-gu because of the cheap prices and the reinforced outer walls made of unique no'orin composites that protected it from the worst of the sonic storms that plagued Órino-Rin more intensely below the meridian. The bar had even served as a storm shelter on more than one occasion. But the prices weren't low enough to bring anyone down here from the upper levels. Especially not soldiers in the employ of the temple. Beni-maru had to have come down seeking something else. Like drugs, or sex or some other illicit vice. But he didn't seem like the type for such things.

"What do you mean?" he asked, gasping, a little out of breath. He was clearly not used to the thicker atmosphere below, despite the air conditioning in the bar.

"You just don't seem like the type that frequents The Mother's Navel," I told him, taking another swig of hoguro. "Now me, I'm here all the time. I live just two levels below. And I've never seen you here before."

"Hmm." He took a few deep, slow breaths. And then, without answering my question, he turned to the server, "One gourd of cold hoguro please. And another for my young friend."

As the server dipped below the bar to retrieve more of the brew, Beni-maru turned back to me, his eyes focused and clear. "It has been so long since we spoke properly. And today when I saw you at the temple again it brought back memories. We didn't really get a chance to catch up. You were just a boy when you left the temple and now, you're a grown man."

He took a long look at me. The din of the bar was loud but not too loud. "Let us drink first, Gwaato. Then we talk."

I briefly entertained the idea that my mother had sent him to make peace. Perhaps she'd reconsidered, had a change of heart and would quietly support my proposal after all. The hoguro had made me optimistic. Too optimistic. I took one of the cold gourds of fresh drink when the server placed them in front of us, poured its cloudy, off-white contents into my smooth clay cup, and took a long deep swallow. Then I waited for Beni-maru to do the same. He only took a small sip of his.

"So, what did you want to talk about?" I asked. Beni-maru and I had been relatively close when I lived at the temple. Or, perhaps not close, but comfortable enough with each other to say we were friends. And while I didn't think of him often after I left, when I did, it was with a kind of misty fondness, like a memory of dew.

“You know, you’re smart. You’ve always been. But when your mother fixed you, she also broke something in you,” he started. Whatever I had been expecting him to say, it certainly wasn’t that.

He continued, “I think she is afraid of your potential and that is why she has always held you back, tried to make you feel small. Or at least smaller than she is.”

Surprise, and a mouthful of hoguro, kept me silent as he went on.

“I was there when she brought you to the temple, you know. It was just my third juzu working there but even then, I knew it wasn’t right, the way she held you, looked at you. I’ve seen my sister with her own children, and I could tell there was something missing in your mother’s eyes. She didn’t want a child; she wanted a devotee, an assistant she could cast into the shape she wanted. I see how she treats you. Talks to you. It has always been the same. She is eager and excited to see your intellectual potential flare up because in a way, she believes it is partly her doing, but at the same time she is always quick to snuff it out when it threatens to become brighter than hers.”

The fleshy side of my face tingled with a rush of blood, and I held my hand up to the other side, the one covered with metal.

When I was seven, I had tried to escape from the orphanage by climbing out of the window of the dormitory I shared with forty-eight other boys, a window overlooking the meridian clouds. I don’t know exactly why but I thought that if I could climb high enough, to the top of the city, that The Mother Goddess would see me, and I could ask her to reunite me with my birth parents whom the Silent Sisters that ran the orphanage had informed me were dead. It was foolish yes, but I had squeezed through the bars and climbed out, digging my tiny fingers into the spaces between the rocks and hauling myself up, through the near-meridian fog of Moki-gu. I thought I was making good progress until my fingers slipped and I fell, cracking my skull against the hard earth of the courtyard.

I was in a coma for three months. At the time, my mother had been working on soundcode for a simulation of the formation of the universe and some of her subroutines had been so innovative and complex that they were being adopted in several other fields, including neuroscience. It was her soundcode that was used to create the neuroprosthesis that replaced my damaged prefrontal cortex and gave me back much of my cognitive function.

I remember seeing her face for the first time when I opened my eyes. She was sandwiched between the shoulders of two tall men—members of the team of uroh-ogi and maadiregi that had saved my life. I noticed her because she was the only one who didn't smile. Her eyes were bright and inquisitive though, focused on me with the intensity of a blast furnace. Her short and curly hair scattered the light from behind her into something like a halo. A luminous crown. She could have been an angel.

The news of my recovery made her even more famous than she'd already been in academic circles. She became a household name. The one whose genius not only explained how the world worked and the mechanisms by which The Mother Goddess had animated the universe but had also saved the life of a desperate orphan. She was appointed to a seat at the council, which she accepted, and she formally adopted me when I was released from the care of the uroh-ogis at the Fehinti'ti treatment center.

"I think she took you in not because of love, but because she saw you as something she could control," Beni-maru said when I didn't respond. "To her, you will always be the poor little broken orphan she fixed."

Even though I knew that most of what he was saying was true, it hurt to hear it. To know that her lack of motherly love for me was so plain, so obvious, that it could be seen from outside our relationship by an external observer. A dense and visible absence, like a black hole at the center of a galaxy.

"I understand exactly who I am to her," I said, perhaps a bit too defensively. "I don't need you to remind me."

"Good." Beni-maru nodded. "It's good to know the truth of things. Even when that truth is bitter."

"So why are you bringing all this up now?"

Beni-maru looked around the bar like he was scanning the room for something and then said, "Because it's important. I need you to know that I understand your position. And I need to be sure you are clear that you don't owe her anything before I go any further. Do you understand that?"

I nodded, already suspicious that he was going to ask me to betray her even if I didn't know exactly how. I felt a tightness in my chest, like the air in the bar had suddenly changed.

There was more to my relationship with my mother than what Beni-maru had outlined. Despite bitter memories of her persistent disapproval, she'd raised me. Fed me. Taught me to recite equations that described all the wonderful and strange ways the universe worked. Hugged me. Sung me to sleep on nights when the wind howled, and the sky roared. Told me stories of The Mother Goddess. Kissed my forehead. Held my hand in darkness. These memories too were layered in the geology of our relationship like bright white marble intercalations. Perhaps they were the reasons I kept trying to get her approval, why I had gone up to the temple today. But no more. Today had been the last time. So, I told Beni-maru firmly, "I understand my position. I have already completely cut ties with her. And I owe her nothing."

"Then we have an understanding." He flashed a smile briefly, the lines of his face deepening, like mudcracks against his dark skin. And then, "The proposal you submitted to the council, the one you spoke to your mother about today. Is it real?"

"Yes," I said, suddenly full of renewed hoguro-induced hope at hearing my proposal mentioned. I didn't even ask him how he'd overheard our conversation since he was supposed to have left the room, left us in privacy. It was becoming increasingly clear to me that Beni-maru was more than just a friendly temple guard.

"Are you sure?" he asked. Something about the way he leaned in and gripped his cup as he asked made me realize the seriousness of the situation.

"As certain as I can be about anything. I've been working on the design since I left the temple. I have thought about it in detail for many juzu. It will work. You said it yourself. I'm smart."

Beni-maru laughed and pressed down the front of his red boubou with hard, firm hands. "Good. Because I know someone that is willing to give you all the resources you need to build your vessel and fund your expedition below the yededek'iyan," he said, eyes narrowing to slits.

"Not the council?"

"No." He shook his head. "Not the council. Or anyone affiliated with the temple. No one there will even talk to you. Your mother has made sure of that."

"Then who?" I asked, concern nipping at my mind like small carnivorous fish.

"Finish your hoguro. I will take you to them."

I regretted how much I'd drunk already but I didn't want him to pick up on my change of demeanor. On my eagerness and fear. So, I held the gourd with both hands to hide the fact that they were trembling and made a show of drinking it, like I was taking a swig when I only took a short sip.

"I'm done." I lied, pushing the half-full cup back toward the young server who gave me a brief, confused look but took it away anyway.

Beni-maru stood up, thin, wiry limbs peeking out of the folds of his boubou like curious tree branches. He put down four owo notes, more than enough to pay for our drinks, and made for the exit.

I followed him out of The Mother's Navel, and into the greenish haze of Órino-Rin's transition zone—the region between the meridian and the yededek'iyan. Visibility was poor and we could only see a half-dozen steps or so ahead of us at a time. Thick olive-colored clouds clung to sides of the mountain face and the perfect cuboid exterior of the elevator. Beni-maru put on his breathing apparatus but I didn't put on mine. I didn't need it. Not for brief exposures anyway. In the distance, I saw streaks of white and blue light chase each other through the clouds and the air around us seemed to rumble. A sonic storm was coming. A small one.

We went to the elevator, and he paid the fare for us to enter one of its dozen pods. The thick doors shut with a metal groan. The elevator pod rose, and we rode it silently, the haze thinning and visibility steadily improving until we were back above the meridian.

A tapestry of stars poked through smooth sky that had been stained pink by the setting of the two suns, and the sweep of clouds dropped away below us in all directions. I could finally see outside as we whizzed past other elevators and rocky outcrops and the smattering of small stocky trees that grew all along the upper slopes of the mountain-continent, their leaves bright green and their trunks scarred from tapping to make hoguro. In the distance, the spires and towers of Mogi-ku and Laima'farwa'wa and all the other mountain-continent cities stood erect, stabbing their dark silhouettes into the sky.

"Beautiful, isn't it?" Beni-maru asked.

"Yes," I replied. Such sunset views were impossible below the meridian, and I had almost forgotten how spectacular they could be.

We exited the elevator onto a wide-open ledge surrounded by craggy, angry-edged rocks on all sides. On the flat ground around us lay scree and an assortment of cables, wires, flat sheets, and incomplete sections of spires like deconstructed millipedes. It was a city maintenance station. It looked abandoned. Sitting right on the lip of the ledge, where the flat ground gave way to dizzying escarpment, an old Tanti'ti shack sat like a giant spider. I froze for a moment. Tanti'ti shacks were traditional nomadic Ts'jenene flying homes and transports. Used to travel the short distances between the mountaintop cities and the less inhabitable mountain peaks of Órino-Rin. A Tanti'ti would never survive a flight below or even close to the meridian, but up here, up high, where the atmosphere was lighter and less temperamental, their manipulation of warm air buoyancy and winds was enough to get them where they needed to go. The Mother's truth be told, my buoyancy adjustment vessel design had been partially inspired by the working mechanism of Tanti'ti shacks.

"Where are you taking me?" I asked Beni-maru, who was already moving confidently toward the shack.

"Up," he said without looking back. "Where we can be sure no one will see or hear us. Don't worry, we are not leaving Mogi-ku. Just floating above it. Your potential patron likes privacy."

There was something different about Beni-maru now. We had crossed some threshold and our relationship had permanently changed; I could sense that. But I retained enough childhood memories of our times together to trust him. Ignoring the dread that was growing in the pit of my stomach as the hoguro slowly cleared its way out of my system, beading my forehead and my back with sweat, I followed him to the perched Tanti'ti shack.

It was mostly white, with a solid black and red pattern of dots, waveforms and ovals ringing its lower parts—a traditional design—just above the soft curve at the base of its conical top, where the six metal legs extended out to grip the ledge, like an insect. A rectangle of red light blinked steadily just above the pattern band like a twitching eye and when we reached the shack, the light turned bright green. A door slid open, and we entered.

The walls were lined with a complex arrangement of pneumatics—metal pipes, fiber tethers, glass tubes, and large leather air bladders that were steadily inflating and deflating like the shack itself was breathing. Circular viewports punctuated the busy walls. The pneumatic arrangements converged at a point, the pilot's standing station directly opposite the entrance, which was slightly lowered with a wide window and a control console in front of it. The pilot was a tall and unusually skinny young woman dressed in traditional Ts'jenene blue and brown leather tunic, trousers, and headscarf. Bright blue tribal marks ran all along her exposed forearms. She didn't turn to look at us, focused instead on the window ahead. But I could tell she was not the one we had come to see.

There was another woman sitting on the floor at the center of the shack, an aura of casual intensity about her. She was wearing a flowing white sleeveless dress that showed off her arms; the toned, muscled arms of someone that had grown up doing manual labor. The dress was of the same pattern as the band outside the shack. Dots, waveforms, and ovals arranged in some symbolic way, their black and red colors stark against the white material. Her head was shaved clean and daubed with ash, and her eyes shone like diamonds even though the area around them was darkened by thick eye shadow. She didn't look like a Ts'jenene nomad.

Beni-maru quietly sat down on the floor, crossing his legs and I followed suit. The woman on the floor snapped her fingers and the skinny pilot responded, adjusting something at the controls with long tentacle-like arms. There was a click and a whoosh and a series of small movements all along the walls as the pipes vibrated and the air bladders around us inflated.

I tried not to show my panic when I felt the shack lift off, leaning to one side before returning to even keel, drifting steadily like pollen in a garden of rock. I was entirely at their mercy. Through the port holes, the sky was clear.

It was only when we were airborne that the sitting woman finally spoke.

"Kanje e bu Ya'yn mara."

"Kanje e bu," I greeted back.

"You don't know me, but I know you. So, allow me to make things balanced. My name is Ochoyo-Tananari," she said with the calm confidence of someone used to recognition by reputation.

And she was right. I recognized the family name. The Kin-Ochoyo clan was a rival to the Kin-Kali family's sonic-storm mining monopoly. The Kin-Ochoyo did not have the resources to set up research temples like the Kin-Kali did, but they had their own ways of conducting research and development and gaining a competitive edge. Like spies. Spies, I now understood, like Beni-maru. I shot him a look, but he didn't return it, focused instead on the pilot.

"And that is Njeriri," Ochoyo-Tananari added, angling her head toward the pilot who gave a single, stiff wave without turning around. The veins on the back of her hand and forearm were so prominent, they looked like a strange roadmap.

"So," Ochoyo-Tananari continued. "I wanted to speak with you because Beni-maru tells me that you have devised a way to descend below the yededek'iyan without destroying yourself. Is that true?"

"Yes," I replied nervously.

"And you need resources to build it."

I confirmed that too.

"Then it seems The Mother may have aligned our interests. My family and I have been developing something special of our own. Tell me, what do you know of sonic storm mining?"

I knew enough of the general principles even though it was not my area of expertise.

"I know it's hard and dangerous to extract the energy from the storms," I told her. "And I know that the Kin-Kali use devices that can absorb the vibrational energy produced by the storms by using synthetic materials whose resonant frequency has been calibrated to match the storms. Once absorbed, the sonic energy can be transferred and stored in special crystals."

"Ririni crystals," she interjected.

"Yes. Thank you. Ririni crystals."

And then rolled her finger, which I took to mean that she wanted me to go on.

"The crystals are easy to transport and use in different applications because of their high energy density per unit volume."

When I paused, she rolled her finger again.

"Apparently, there used to be people who mine sounds from the sonic storms without any equipment," I added. "People who could survive direct exposure to sonic storms and even channel some of a storm's power directly to Ririni crystals."

"There are," she corrected. "Conductives. The Ts'jenene call them Iji-omoji. The children of the storm. The ones whose inner fragment of Mothersound, the sound that animates all things, hums close to the natural frequency of sonic storms. They are rare now. Or at least only a few of them are known. There was a time when Iji-omoji used to be kidnapped and forced into servitude, mining sonic energy. But that was long before the vibrational panel technology was developed. Things are far more civilized now. A few of them remain a ceremonial part of the sound mining process in some areas, others wander the skies, helping small communities but they mostly keep a low profile."

"I see."

Her stare indicated to me that she still wanted me to continue.

"I have heard that the naturally occurring Ririni crystals can hold immense amounts of energy in the structure of their lattices. Estimates of their storage capacity vary widely. Some maadiregi theorize that some crystals can hold more energy than the twin suns release in a hundred juzu without shattering."

"Ah! Not that again. It is gba'agbo. Not ii-mo. And not even good gba'agbo at that. An extrapolation from one single study that used a questionable methodology which some maadiregi got carried away by," she said, smiling at Beni-maru. "But yes, it is true that some crystals have been used to store all the energy from multiple storms without any damage to their structural integrity. Still, it is difficult to test them to their limits, as you can probably understand."

"Indeed, I do," I replied.

She twirled her finger again, but I had told all I knew. So, I bowed my head, waiting for her. A silence swelled to fill the pause as the Tanti'ti shack hovered steadily over the mountain continent. The pilot was good. Very good. I barely even noticed any movements as I had on previous Tanti'ti flights.

Finally, Ochoyo-Tananari said, "You know enough about how sound mining works to understand what I am about to tell you. The key limitations of sonic storm mining are not in storing the energy, but in predicting where and when the storms will occur and how much energy they contain, and in building a device that can vibrate at the right frequency long enough and stably enough to transfer all that energy to a Ririni crystal without being destroyed." She leaned forward. "Up here, it's nice and safe for us to live because the storms are relatively weak and infrequent despite their almost aleatory nature. The strongest storms that those of you who live near the meridian experience might release enough energy to destroy a small, unprotected settlement, but that is barely enough energy to power a small industrial complex. Not even enough to launch a small probe beyond the gravitational grip of our planet. And the Kin-Kali almost always beat us to them." She looked at Beni-maru and her upper lip tightened. "But the storms below the yededek'iyan are much more powerful, much more destructive. They release so much more energy in a single occurrence. Those are the most valuable storms. Those are the storms we want to extract sonic energy from."

She paused again, allowing the implication to sink in. The intensity of her gaze was all-consuming, like fire.

"I see," I said because I finally understood what she wanted. Why she had asked Beni-maru to bring me here. The Kin-Kali were very good at predicting storm occurrences and arriving before anyone else could. The army of researchers at the temple of unbroken light, my mother among them, had made sure of that, with major advances in sonic storm forecasting using detailed soundcode that ran complex probabilistic mathematical models of Órino-Rin's geodynamics. The same base soundcode that had given me my cognitive function back, after the fall.

It seemed Kin-Ochoyo was taking a different approach. No longer trying to beat the Kin-Kali at their own game. They wanted to change the game completely.

"We have developed a new type of resistant vibration panel that can absorb and transfer energy to the Ririni crystals rapidly so that they don't get overloaded and destroyed while vibrating at sonic storm frequencies. But we need to test them on a large enough storm. A supermassive storm of the kind that only occurs below the yededek'iyan. One that holds enough energy to power all the cities on Órino-Rin for a whole juzu, perhaps more. Do you understand?"

I knew Ochoyo-Tananari didn't care what lay below or what the surface of the planet was like, or even if it had one at all. About whether my mother was right or wrong. She didn't care about any of my academic curiosities. About ii-mo or gba'agbo. She only cared about her sound mining business. About getting a competitive advantage. About winning. She was focused on only one goal. I could see it in her eyes because I had seen the same look in mine. I recognized it. That need that had set deep into my bones.

The familiar tingle where the flesh and metal parts of my face met returned. It was the excitement. Excitement at the opportunity to finally build the buoyancy adjustment vessel I had been dreaming of for so long. And I knew that if this worked, the Kin-Kali would lose their iron grip on the city and my mother would lose her position, her funding, her prestige. I wanted nothing more than to see my device work, to be hailed as the visionary, the explorer. I could already imagine my mother's face when she heard the news of what I had done and, I am ashamed to say, the thought gave me pleasure. The all-consuming desire to achieve something significant that would wipe away decades of my mother's disappointments swelled. I was going to do it by surpassing her. I would do what she could not. Maybe then she would see how wrong she'd been about me.

"Yes," I said, using as few words as I could to choke back the flood of emotions swirling behind my throat. "I understand."

"Excellent. Then we are aligned in our purpose. We will give you all you need to build and test your vessel. Beni-maru will oversee this effort—we have other eyes and ears in the temple of unbroken light, and besides, I trust him more than anyone else to manage this."

Beside me, Beni-maru nodded quietly. I knew that by *to manage this* she really meant *to manage you*. But I didn't care.

"Once your vessel is functional, we will use it to descend as far as is possible below the yededek'iyan and test our new vibrational absorption panels there."

"I agree. On one condition," I said, trying to sound as confident as I could.

She cocked her head. "Condition? What condition?"

"I want to go. On the descent mission. I need to see." I needed to obtain firsthand ii-mo to displace my mother's gba'agbo.

She shook her head. "No. You are more valuable to me up here. In case something goes wrong, and we need to rebuild."

"Nothing will go wrong," I insisted.

"And you are willing to bet your life on that?"

"I am. I have been designing this system for many juzu. I have thought of everything. And we will test it before manning it to be sure." My nervousness had been completely replaced by that intense desire. The same need that had been driving me to study relentlessly, to recite calculations long into the night in my squalid sub-meridian home, trying to come up with some innovation or discovery that would surpass my mother. The same desire that had driven me to climb out of the orphanage window and up the cliff trying to show myself to the Mother Goddess so that perhaps she would see me and hear me and maybe bring my parents back.

"I must go." I closed my eyes and inhaled deeply. "I need this. Please."

Ochoyo-Tananari stared at me silently with her star-bright eyes for a moment and then looked away to the side. I followed her gaze and through the porthole I saw the blur of snowy mountain peaks drifting by. Njeriri had flown the Tanti'ti shack high up towards the upper edge of the mountain range that hosted Mogi-ku. The jagged brown peaks stood solemn, a shadow cast on the side closest to us, hidden from the light of the twin suns.

When Ochoyo-Tananari turned back to me, the space between her eyes furrowed and her tone lowered.

"Fine. You will go. But only when I am reasonably confident your vessel works."

"Thank you." I bowed low, touching the cool floor of the shack with my forehead to show my gratitude.

She leaned forward. "Do not disappoint me."

It was not a request.

Part Two: Fall

The dream of breaking the veil of the yededek'iyan had taken me to the edge of my sanity. The effort and the cost had been greater than I or Ochoyo-Tananari anticipated. But after eight months of calculation songs, prototyping, soundcoding, design revisions, construction, and rigorous testing, we were finally ready to sink into our planet's unforgiving lower roil in our cocoon of hard-won technological armor.

The four of us chosen by Ochoyo-Tananari to go below stood atop the brightly lit cliff on the western edge of the city, behind a field of spires rising through thin clouds. Beni-maru, Njeriri and a tall and bulky Aq'pa named Ráxaxar whose large claws, poking out of his webbed hands and feet, made me uncomfortable.

The bright edge of the Juah-āju's rising upper disk was already visible. It was almost first sunrise. The vessel I had dreamed of for so long and birthed into reality by force of will and an abundance of Kin-Ochoyo funds stood in front of us, set against the young light.

It was a gleaming white assembly of two triple-hulled, no'orin composite spheres attached to each other by a thick, short cylindrical pipe and three equidistant solid struts that ran tangential to both spheres. The entire vessel stood exactly twenty-two meters high and seven across—the same as the diameter of each sphere, and the struts extended a half meter below to form a triangle of three retractable short legs on which the entire assembly stood. Ochoyo-Tananari had said it looked like an hourglass when she first saw it and while I didn't get what she meant at first, because I thought she was simply reminding me of how much of her time and money I had consumed to create it, I eventually saw the resemblance.

A system of thirty-six ports and vents pockmarked the surface of both spheres—to manage the internal pressure and buoyancy of the assembly by controlling the ratio of atmospheric gas between the spaces of the three hulls. Every element of the structure was made of no'orin composites created using a unique process I invented—layering long-chained no'orin polymer in nanometer-thick membranes to each other via hydrogen bonding until they were solid, impermeable slabs with strengths more than a hundred times that of any other no'orin composite. To rupture the hull would require not just enough energy to rip the individual molecular strands apart, but also to overcome the incredible intermolecular bonds holding the entire polymer bundle together like an army of overprotective mothers. It would take an incredibly powerful sonic storm of the sort that had only ever been theorized by the maadiregi to even make a dent.

The autocatalytic templating mechanism I used to achieve the planar structure of the no'orin polymer and give it the proper orientation to enforce its structure had required the construction of an expensive custom factory beneath the Kin-Ochoyo sonic energy transport facilities, but I was sure it would make Ochoyo-Tananari very rich once she and her other maadiregi found a way to scale it up. Not as rich as they would be if their vibrational panel worked, but enough to relieve the pressure of the entire enterprise's expense on me just a bit.

The material engineering had been difficult and expensive, but it was the design of the control system for the triple hull that had been the most complex aspect of the construction, soundcoding each to semi-automatically channel the air at the right flow rate and temperature on command from the pilot, while absorbing the impact of winds and storms. We'd spent thousands of hours on fine-tuning it. I'd sung every equation until they were a constant chorus in my head. Tested it in every condition we could simulate. It was ready. I was sure.

"Let's go," Beni-maru said, stepping forward.

Njeriri grunted and walked quickly, moving ahead with steady steps, as if she was eager to enter the vessel she was going to pilot. I couldn't read her expression though. Her long hair was braided close to her scalp like the crop rows that grew in the soil-and-volcanic-ash-filled flank craters of Moki-gu. Her eyes were sunken, but clear, making her seem even more gaunt than her barely concealed drug habit usually did. Her family was Ts'jenene, which was how she'd become expert at piloting—by illegally racing Tanti'ti shacks close to the meridian. They used to be rich, until poor choices and unpaid loans had driven them from the nomad skies, down into the bowels of Mogi-ku and sent her into a drug habit she had still not escaped.

Ráxaxar followed close behind her, carrying a heavy black box, his long talons pressing against its base. The Aq'pa are strong, very strong but hardly ever interact with humans. Amphibious, with gills in front of their chests that ran all the way up to their necks, and bodies covered in thick brown scales, they were indigenous to this planet and were here on Órino-Rin long before our ancient ancestors arrived. Most of them lived below the meridian. Ráxaxar didn't speak at all, he only ever communicated in sign with Beni-maru and Njeriri, and I still wasn't sure why exactly Ochoyo-Tananari wanted him to come with us, except to haul the precious vibrational panel cargo. She'd said he was a sonic storm mining technician who would help Beni-maru run the test when we had descended far enough, but the lifting and lowering of the panels could have been automated. I'd even offered to design a mechanism to do it, but Beni-maru and Ochoyo-Tananari had declined, and then refused to tell me why.

As we walked toward the vessel, Beni-maru raised his hand and gave the signal for the Tanti'ti carrier that would drop us over the cliff edge to get prepared. Somewhere behind all the activity on the cliff, I knew Ochoyo-Tananari was watching.

We entered the bottom sphere of the vessel, one by one, its air-tight door sliding up to let us in like a theatre curtain going up to reveal a stage. Inside, it was an open chamber with the upper sphere forming a top dome and a flat elevated floor on which there were four stations with chairs facing each other and straps to hold us down. The chairs could be rotated with a mechanism to lock them in place if needed. Between each station, there were atmospheric exposure suits with air tanks attached, in case of emergency. Each suit had been custom designed to fit our body shapes, one for each crew member. They stood upright, held up by suspension hooks and supported by a series of buckles to keep them in place along the curved wall of the vessel. The space was illuminated by a ring of lights. It was clear and clean, the complex network of circuits, cables, motors, gears, and valves that made everything work was hidden beneath the floor and behind the smooth white walls. It made the miracle of what we had achieved appear almost mundane.

"This is your doing, Gwaato. You made something spectacular here. You should be proud of yourself," Beni-maru said, patting my shoulder as Ráxaxar set down the black box he was carrying next to his chair and latched it into place.

Surprised, I simply said, "Thank you," and smiled at Beni-maru as we sat down in our stations, next to each other. We'd grown closer over the last eight months. He was a quiet and firm but supportive supervisor, always asking more of me but unwavering in his support whenever something went wrong or there was a delay which had to be explained to Ochoyo-Tananari. And he was effusive with praise whenever we hit a new progress milestone. It was obvious he had been wasted as a spy, and I came to know that he had been requesting another assignment for almost three juzu, but they had kept him there waiting for one more morsel of information that was juicy enough to justify his replacement. This wasn't just my opportunity, it was his. His face seemed to radiate something like pride and in that moment, as his look lingered, I half expected him to say something like *your mother would be proud of you.* But he didn't. Because he knew better. And because she wouldn't be. Or would she? I wasn't sure. She'd probably find something to criticize.

I pressed the button to open the window shutters in front of each chair. Natural light flooded into the vessel. Each window was composed of six separate layers of transparent no'orin polymer, including the impact shutters. The inner layer of the windows had been fitted with filters to manipulate the various light spectra from outside, automatically adjusted to give the best resolution possible. Once we were below, the filters would adjust so that we could see as much as possible and navigate our way down. The windows had been the second most complicated thing to design since it had meant putting portholes in the reinforced no'orin shells and every seam and joint and attachment was a potential failure point. But they were important. I needed ii-mo.

Njeriri planted herself in the chair at the station opposite us, next to Ráxaxar, her thin hands wrapped around her body like she was shivering.

"Hey Njeriri, are you good?"

"Fucking perfect," she replied without even looking at me.

"She's always good," Beni-maru said. "I've seen her look worse and still win a Tanti'ti race over the eastern Moki-gu ridge."

She sucked her teeth with a loud, dismissive hiss.

If I hadn't seen her pilot the prototype effortlessly—like it was an extension of her own body—during our testing phase, I would have been concerned. Still, I was glad we wouldn't need her to take control of the descent until the Tanti'ti carrier dropped us.

"All systems live," Beni-maru said, initiating the pre-launch checks.

Njeriri, Ráxaxar and I turned on the receivers on our ears and ran our fingers over the control panels to feel the vibration of information coming through. The onboard vessel sensors transmitted data to our receivers as direct cochlear transmissions. Velocity, depth, pressure, rotation, buoyancy ratios, temperature, all that we needed to know. We all raised our hands with our index fingers pointed up and other fingers curled back—the Ts'jenene hand signal for "good." Everything was in order.

"Ready for launch," Beni-maru said through the transmitter on the panel in front of him. It would be Ochoyo-Tananari that gave the order. All we had to do was wait until we felt the tug of the carrier.

"Rombo'obo kanakara." *Good luck,* came her voice from the receivers. "And may The Mother bring you back up safely."

"Thank you," I whispered.

Njeriri snorted. "I'm the one bringing us back up, not some imaginary sky-woman."

Beni-maru shook his head at the blasphemy as he replied to Ochoyo-Tananari. "Thank you."

Ráxaxar made a sign with his hands that I did not recognize.

And then, we waited.

The launch was really nothing more than a complicated fall. Three large Tanti'ti carriers, modified for the purpose, navigated to our position, and dropped cables that latched onto the struts of the vessel. They lifted us up from the lip of the cliff and drifted in unison away from the launch station until we were between the two great mountain-continents that hosted Mogi-ku and Laima'farwa'wa, the cities growing on their sides like lichen.

Beni-maru turned to me and indicated my panel with a jut of his jaw. He wanted me to give the final launch request.

A warmth filled my chest as I said, "Ready to drop in three."

There was only the hum of equipment for a moment and through the window, I could see second sunrise beginning. The edge of Zuúv'ah's disk was peeking into the sky, smaller due to its distance, but still blazing light and adding bright yellow streaks to the white light of Juah-āju already shining down on the thick carpet of meridian clouds below.

"Great Mother be with us. May we be instruments of your will," Beni-maru prayed.

Three.

Two.

One.

Into the open space between the mountain cities, above the yawn of cloudy murk below, the carriers let go.

We fell.

Faster and faster, accelerating as gravity seized our bulk. My heart lurched in my chest as the vertical mountain-city swept by in a blur.

We stayed upright and stable because our crew weight served as live ballast and Njeriri was already adjusting the air intake to slow our fall. She activated the heat exchanger to fill the upper sphere with heated air while venting the outer hull of the lower one to give us more buoyancy.

She turned her head from side to side and mumbled to herself as she worked, obviously in her element, enjoying herself, surfing the edge of some arcane high. Beni-maru had closed his eyes, retreating inward. Ráxaxar's face remained an inscrutable mask, the pink gills on his neck throbbing distractingly.

I needed something to focus on, so I turned away and touched the information vibration slab on the control panel to take in the direct cochlear transmission of vessel performance data. The information came like a voice in my head. I took it all in quickly. Radar indicated there was nothing solid within two kilometers of us. Wind speed was moderate, not too high. Pressure was rising. Temperature was dropping. As was our speed.

When it hit a stable, low, terminal velocity that didn't make me feel like my stomach was going to come out of my mouth, I looked up to the display through my window. We were still above the meridian and the city of Mogi-ku looked beautiful in the distance, a smattering of domes and shacks and towers and caves climbing up the mountain like the appendages of some vine-creature. The long line of the central elevator running through it from top to bottom like a vital vein. I could just about make out the sub-meridian part of the city where I lived, where Beni-maru had come to find me in The Mother's Navel. That day seemed so far away now.

When we crossed the meridian, the air changed. A familiar vibration rang through the vessel like a gong, setting my teeth to chatter as we dropped past the critical pressure and temperature of the atmosphere. The light of the two suns dulled and visibility dropped to less than twenty meters as the denser air seized us.

The vessel began to wobble. The wind had picked up and the new air density was throwing us off center.

"We're fine. I've got it under control," Njeriri called out. I could hear her quickly clicking her fingers across the panel to vent air and balance the change in opposing forces that were tugging at us. She muttered an incantation as she worked and there was a subtle glow around her fingers that let me know she was using sound magic to augment her piloting skill.

Soon, we were stable again and falling at a moderate velocity as we had agreed for the altitude between the meridian and the yededek'iyan. The transition zone was troublesome, yes, but not particularly dangerous. Many people lived not far above those depths in the greenish-yellow haze of supercritical air. There was the occasional electric blue flash of a sonic storm and the solid black and brown edge of a rock overhang across the screen, but we continued unmolested by our planet's atmosphere.

Suddenly, there was a loud crack and through all the windows, flashes of lightning like angry blue seams appeared. I knew what it was before we felt it.

"Sonic storm!" I shouted just as we felt the shockwave hit. The release of energy set the vessel vibrating and we began to spin. We were still high up and I was certain our no'orin composites could handle the impact. We just needed our pilot to do the same.

"Got it under control!" Njeriri yelled back, already working with the controls to adjust the thrust of air through the vents. We rode the inconstant amplitude of the storm like it was a wild beast, spinning at an axial tilt for a few seconds. Everything was a blur of cloud and rain and light, and then when the fangs of the storm briefly receded, she rapidly pressurized the upper sphere, reducing our buoyancy. We plunged, back to vertical, and out of the storm, into the sub-meridian haze. My heart thumped wildly in my chest.

"Njeriri, we're falling too fast," Beni-maru said, almost in a whisper.

I gripped my chair and pressed myself into it, praying to The Mother that my design had held, that nothing had been damaged by the storm.

"I said I've got it under control," she insisted, sounding annoyed.

There was the clicking sound of more adjustments, some more urgent incantation, and finally our descent slowed. We stopped carouseling. I let out a deep breath.

"Good work," Beni-maru said to Njeriri, his voice calm, too calm.

"No problem, old timer." There was a venom in her voice that told of the history between them. I knew some of it through rumors at the facility and the half-sentences from a few of Njeriri's drug-addled rants. Njeriri and Beni-maru's nephew had been romantically involved and Beni-maru hadn't approved because of her habit. The way Njeriri told it, it was Beni-maru's words of disapproval, not his sister's, that had made the boy break up with her. She said she didn't care about the boy or the relationship and that she never truly had, but her persistent resentment for Beni-maru indicated otherwise.

Still frazzled, I looked to my side.

Ráxaxar remained silent and his face remained the same. Emotionless. He could have been a statue, the Aq'pa. I wondered what his motivation was for joining us. Aq'pa typically avoided the company of humans. They were the true descendants of Órino-Rin, having evolved on this planet, and they largely resented us for coming to their world and claiming it as ours. Was he an outcast? Did he owe a debt to Ochoyo-Tananari? The inscrutable mask of his face gave no indication.

Through the windows, the visibility kept dropping and my heart was still fluttering so I focused on the windows whose filters had auto-adjusted to infrared displays. There was nothing around us. It was like falling into a dream. A dream of a planet with no solid surface, nothing but a ball of gas with mighty rocks drifting on it like gods swimming an ocean, each breath a sonic storm. Just as my mother had theorized. The screen next to the vibrational panels showed a blinking radar.

Seeing the endless sea of haze, it was easy to believe then that perhaps my mother had been right after all. But the easy thing to believe wasn't always the right thing, the true thing. And no one had seen beyond the veil of atmospheric impossibility. We wouldn't know for sure until we crossed the yededek'iyan. I needed to see for myself, to obtain ii-mo.

We continued to fall.

When we finally crossed the yededek'iyan, it was not obvious.

It's less a well-defined dividing line and more a theoretical smear—a short, extended region that marks the lower boundary of the transition zone. Its exact starting depth varies from place to place and from time to time. The edges of the yededek'iyan are always in flux. Unlike crossing the meridian, there is no noticeable change in atmospheric phase from gas to supercritical fluid which has the density of a liquid but the viscosity of a gas and feels like moving through a particularly thick cloud. Instead, the already-supercritical atmosphere simply reaches a pressure and temperature condition that is impossible to survive in and keeps getting worse. And then there is the exponential increase in sonic storm frequency. You know you have crossed the yededek'iyan when all your protective equipment begins to break down. When you begin to die.

Inside the buoyancy adjustment vessel, the pressure sensor vibrated a warning to my cochlea that indicated we were close to my estimate of where the yededek'iyan would be, at the bisector of the two mountain-continent ranges. The temperature was already far below freezing, and the vessel shuddered frequently like it was suffering a fever. Outside, the world around us was chaos. Carbon dioxide, methane and the thousand other gases that made up the atmosphere whirled and eddied with the wind around us, pelting the windows with condensed droplets of carbonic acid and solid crystalline hydrates. Visibility was nearly zero, all we could see was the white and yellow-ish green of the haze. But I wasn't worried. I had designed the no'orin polymer composites to handle all of that, including the corrosion.

Cocooned in the vessel's warm womb, with Njeriri taking us down slowly like we were a falling bubble, I kept staring at the display screens on the control panel. She had increased the buoyancy in the upper sphere so that we were falling even more slowly, more cautiously, just in case there was a solid, hard surface below, waiting for us to break ourselves on it. But the radar still pinged that there was nothing around us within a two-kilometer radius.

"We have been favored by The Mother," I announced, breaking the long silence since the storm. I turned my chair around and the others followed suit. "We have crossed the yededek'iyan and are now deeper than anyone on Órino-Rin has ever been before."

"Indeed," Beni-maru replied, touching his shoulder with his index finger, the sign of thanks to the mother. "The Mother gave you the wisdom to build this device. It appears she finally wishes for us to fully know the planet she gifted us when she guided our ancestors here from across the stars."

Ráxaxar grunted, turned around and signed a word I did not know. The first thing he'd said to me, and I couldn't understand it.

"Congratulations," Beni-maru translated, seeing the confusion on my face. "He said congratulations."

And then, Ráxaxar moved his hands rapidly as he signed something to Beni-maru, keeping his arms tight to his torso so that he did not expose the sensitive reproductive buds that ran across his side, from the hip to the underarm. The Aq'pa's expression did not change but Beni-maru's did.

"I'm sorry," he said. "I did not mean it like that. Of course, The Mother gifted the world to the Aq'pa and the Tetekute first. You are the ones who evolved here. We did not discover it. I'm sorry if I implied otherwise."

Ráxaxar signed one more word and Beni-maru gave a slight bow.

"Thank you," he said.

Njeriri started to laugh, throwing her hands out to her sides and making a big show of it.

"What's so funny?" Beni-maru asked.

"You." She pointed disrespectfully at Beni-maru with her left hand. "You are funny. Hilarious even. Hypocrisy is always funny when it is exposed."

Beni-maru remained calm. "What are you talking about?"

"You know you and your temple friends don't believe that the Aq'pa and Tetekute truly own this world. You think The Mother led our ancestors to come here and seize this world from them because it was our destiny to rule the stars." She rolled her eyes. "I've heard the jokes and the comments you all make when you think you're alone. But now that Ráxaxar called you out on it, you backtracked. Why don't you say what you truly believe? Say it proud, say it with your chest."

"I don't think any of those things. I respect the first people of this world."

"Liar." She said the word like she was spitting at him.

Beni-maru flinched. "I am not a liar."

Njeriri laughed her scornful laugh again. "You think you're so clever, so much better than the rest of us. But you aren't. You pretended to be an honorable man while you spied on your employers at the temple of unbroken light, betraying their trust for more than a decade. You say you don't meddle in other people's affairs and yet you poison other people's relationships. You privately despise the Aq'pa, calling them primitive and inferior while you pretend to be Ráxaxar's friend, smiling to his face. You are a hypocrite."

Beni-maru shook his head. "I don't know how much of that filth you put in your body today of all days, but I think it's starting to affect your judgment."

"Oh please. As if you never experimented with drugs or drank some hoguro to help you deal with a difficult situation. The drugs aren't doing anything except making me feel good and dampening my anxiety to make me a more effective pilot. My hands are steady, as is my mind. You know that." She held her hands out to him as if challenging him to inspect them. "And yeah, I am an addict, so what? That has nothing to do with what I am talking about now. I'm just tired of your hypocritical shit, that's all."

Beni-maru's left eye twitched and anger briefly flashed across his face. "That's enough."

But she didn't stop. "You're not better than any of us. We are all just people—human, Aq'pa, Tetekute, whatever—we're complicated pieces of biological material that are neither good nor bad, just trying to make meaning of this messed up world and make the best choices we can at the time and find things and people that love us, which we can love back. Nothing wrong with that. But you don't accept that. You think you can pass judgment on people when you're just another piece of Dwandeki shit like everyone else. The only problem I have with you is that you won't admit it to yourself."

Beni-maru did not respond. But his fists were clenched so tight his knuckles were pale.

Njeriri sucked her teeth with disdain and then turned to me. "Yay for you, Gwaato, you crossed your precious yededek'iyan."

I could tell she didn't care at all.

"I hope it's all you expected it to be. Just don't trust this one." She indicated Beni-maru with a jut of her jaw. "He will say whatever he thinks you need to hear to convince you to do what he wants, what's best for him. Remember he lied to your mother's face for more than a decade."

"Njeriri, that's enough. I hope you got out whatever you feel you needed to. But we have a job to do." Beni-maru's calm had returned.

"See what I said? He'll say and do anything to get what he wants. Even swallow my insults."

Njeriri raised her hands in mock surrender and glared at Beni-maru for a moment before deciding that it actually was enough.

She signed something to Ráxaxar and he responded with a single sign that had all the communication complexity of a shrug.

Then Ráxaxar signed more words, this time at Beni-maru.

"He is asking how much further you want to drop before we test the vibrational panels," Njeriri translated for me.

I looked to Beni-maru but he looked back to me and said, "As deep as Gwaato says we can go. His design. His vessel. His call."

I thought about it for a moment, still rattled by her outburst. "We planned to go as far as possible. To the surface, if there is one. That was the agreement with Ochoyo-Tananari."

"But we can't just keep descending forever, can we?" Njeriri translated Ráxaxar's rapid hand gestures. "We need to test the panels."

"The deepest probe that has ever been dropped below the yededek'iyan gave out at about fifty kilometers below the meridian. We are now deeper than that." I replied, voice trembling. "By my estimates, if there is a low-density core with a solid surface, it should appear between sixty-five and eighty kilometers below, depending on the density gradient."

Ráxaxar grunted and signed again. More forceful this time.

"How far?" Njeriri translated again, returning her focus to Beni-maru.

"It's Gwaato's call," he repeated firmly.

I decided to end it. "We can deploy the panels and test them at seventy-five kilometers below if we haven't reached a solid surface yet."

She looked from him to me, laughed and said, "I hope you know what you are doing, because he is only letting you decide so that if something goes wrong, he can blame it on you," then she turned back to the control panel.

"What's her problem? She seems more agitated than usual," I whispered to Beni-maru when things were quiet again. I tried to mask my concern with a cavalier tone but Beni-maru simply shook his head and turned back to his panel.

I did the same, hoping that the tension between them would stay contained for the remainder of the mission. The last thing we needed was to fight each other at a critical moment.

For a few minutes, it was quiet in the vessel. There was nothing but the low thrum of the heat exchanger and air filter, the low, steady pinging of the vessel's vibration and the occasional rustle of clothing when someone adjusted position in their chair.

We continued to drop through the dream of clouds like an insect swimming between two gods. Closing my eyes, I took deep breaths and tried to clear my head of the turmoil Njeriri had planted by imagining what the surface of the world would look like, feel like, if we reached it. Would it be muddy soil? Some solid, crystalized form of the atmospheric gas mix? Smooth wet rock like the mountain-continents, with supercritical fluid adsorbed onto its surface? There were so many possibilities. And then I tried to imagine what my mother would say when I described it to her, this surface she'd said didn't exist. How she would react when I told her I had seen it with my own eyes.

A question from Njeriri suddenly penetrated the silence, “Why in the name of The Mother is atmospheric density falling?”

I opened my eyes to see what was happening outside. The hazy gas around us was thinning rapidly. Visibility was rising and I saw flashes of light in the distance.

I turned around. Saw Njeriri’s fingers do their practiced dance across the slick white control panel to slow our descent. She seemed genuinely frazzled for the first time since we started. And she kept repeating, “It doesn’t make sense,” over and over like it was a temple mantra or a prayer.

I touched the slab on the control panel, and it vibrated a warning to my cochlea that the atmospheric density was now about eighty percent of the expected value for this depth.

Njeriri was right, it didn’t make sense.

Outside the vessel, the thinning haze loomed but breaking beneath was a sea of bright light rushing up to meet us.

“What is that?” Beni-maru asked and a frisson of fear-tinged excitement surged through me because I had no idea. Everywhere on Órino-Rin, we had observed that atmospheric density increased with depth. There were no known exceptions. This inversion was an anomaly.

When we fell out of the bottom of the haze and into the light, I was seized by a deep and profound awe.

Visibility exploded out to hundreds of meters. I saw two towering throats of hard, brown and black and jagged rock, swallowed by two decks of haze—the yellow-green upper deck we had come through and an inscrutable gray, like gigantic dark rainclouds, below.

Njeriri gasped.

It was a vista of lovely desolation. These were the lower regions of the mountain continents that held up our home cities, tall and wide and yet so small set against the anomalous atmospheric cavern we’d fallen into. They looked like pillars set between two skies to hold them. Just like the struts that kept the upper and lower spheres of our vessel together. For a moment, I could not tell which direction was up or down and a rush of vertigo overtook my mind like a cup of fresh hoguro.

“Great Mother!” Beni-maru exclaimed.

Ráxaxar didn’t react audibly. I expected that the wonder of what we were witnessing would be enough to change his usual unflappable demeanor. But it was not.

The alarms were screaming that the temperature had shot up by more than a hundred degrees even though the pressure remained mostly the same. It had to be some kind of thermal anomaly that had warmed the air above the critical temperature, sending it back into the vapor phase but the atmosphere was still so dense that refracted light made the horizon curve upward like an unexpected smile.

Along the surface of the two mountain continents, there were gleaming red volcanic fractures vomiting black sulfuric smoke and lava domes seeping magma like blood. Gigantic frothy geysers of yellow vapor were erupting into the sky. The vapors arched high and when they fell, they dissipated before touching the lower deck of haze below, like a painting of a waterfall that the artist had abandoned before finishing. A raging flow of giant disappearing springs.

It was a part of Órino-Rin no one had ever seen before. No one had even theorized such a layer of our atmosphere. It was spectacular. It was terrifying. And we were the first to witness its glory.

"Brace yourselves!" Njeriri shouted as we fell out of the thermal inversion layer and into the gray sea of haze below. The vessel groaned with the sudden spike of density and temperature. The windows displayed nothing but dark clouds bruising the world and a maelstrom of blue-white lightning. We'd been so distracted by the planet's beauty that we'd forgotten its danger. We'd fallen right into another sonic storm. A supermassive one. A terrifying turbulence seized our vessel and set us tumbling wildly, losing all sense of direction, of control.

My heart lurched madly in my chest with each sudden change in direction and orientation, following the whims of the sonic storm. We couldn't hear it, but we could feel it unleashing its fury against the vessel. My teeth chattered and I could hear my blood pounding its way through my body. A feeling like the prelude to a scream pervaded my senses but terror froze my lungs with an icy grip. My body jerked madly against the harness and the vessel shuddered ceaselessly. The temperature swing, the density change, and the sonic storm hit us at the same time. Njeriri could not react quickly enough, even with sound magic spurring her fingers on.

We were in freefall.

The filters of the windows couldn't keep up and everything was a blur. Screens were flickering. Alarms were blaring. The world was spinning. The vessel was groaning. Our bodies were straining. We were all screaming and even Raxaxar was screeching a horrible sound that made me feel faint and made my eyes water. I couldn't breathe.

"Parachute! Now!" Njeriri cried out.

In the chaos, I caught sight of Beni-maru pressing the button on his panel to deploy the emergency parachute. A thin sheet of n'orin composite that would hopefully spread out and slow our fall.

We jerked hard against the pull of gravity and were violently reoriented. But only for a second. Not enough time for Njeriri to take control of our descent, only enough for us to be hit by another sonic storm. I felt the lurch as the parachute's drag gave out, but my heart didn't truly sink until I heard the low whoosh of gas leaking. There'd been a hull rupture. That was supposed to be impossible. Unless the material connection points for my no'orin composite structure had failed. But how? I'd designed them to handle even the most powerful theorized storms. Was this a storm more powerful than any we'd imagined? Or was there some error in my design? I didn't know. And with the seal of the vessel broken, our protection from external sound waves rendered imperfect, I could finally hear a muted version of the fury of the storm outside, and it was like the entire planet was screaming at us. If we heard the fullness of it, we would be deafened forever.

"I can't slow it down!" Njeriri yelled over the cacophony, still frantically trying to rebalance the gas volumes to account for the leak.

Raxaxar leaned over his chair and was holding onto the energy vibrational panel tight like his life depended on it. Beni-maru dug his fingers into the armrests of his chair.

"Brace!" he shouted. And then I heard him say something that sounded like, "Blessed Mother, have mercy on us," but I couldn't be sure. Everything was too loud. Everything was too much.

Gritting my teeth, I tasted iron on my tongue. I kept willing myself not to pass out as we hurtled down, lashed on all sides by the rage of the supermassive sonic storm.

Something slammed into the vessel with the force of a scorned god's vengeance. The sound was so loud that I could barely hear myself screaming over the cacophonous violence of no'orin polymer composite groaning, glass shattering, metal screeching. The smell of smoke seeped up from my control panel. When darkness finally invaded my consciousness, I was sure we were all dead.

Part Three: Descent

In the darkness, I dream of flight.

And I dream of my mother.

In this dream, we are flying at an angle through the pallid haze, ice frosting the tips of our wings. We only stop flying when we burst through the curtain of dense atmosphere into the wondrous beauty of the thermal inversion. We swoop down in wide arcs towards the pillars of the world, the bright red lava and the thick black smoke and wispy yellow vapors erupting from their rock-skin.

"It's beautiful," she tells me. "I could have never imagined anything like it."

I smile until my heart becomes a flower. I reach into my chest and pluck it out, a bright red hibiscus the color of blood.

She takes it and kisses my forehead.

We continue to fly.

We follow the curve of a mountain continent, peeking into the deep rocky caverns and tunnels that pockmark its surface. We fly, descending until we are under the arc of a hot geyser, and then we touch the surface of a lava lake as we glide low. We fly and we fly, and we twist, and we loop. She starts to laugh and laugh and laugh and then she flies right up to me and hugs me and tells me that she loves me and that she is proud of me and that I was right all along to come here, to use my restored mind independently, to think beyond her geodynamic theories, to seek ii-mo. I cry. My tears fall and become birds that sing a song she'd taught me when she first adopted me. A song about how The Mother made the universe, sculpting the formlessness of unreality like clay until it was a new and beautiful thing. Our embrace lasts forever. When she lets go of me, she beams a smile, spreads her wings gracefully and flutters upward, until she catches an updraft and soars back into the upper deck of haze, back toward Mogi-ku. The birds that were my tears ascend with her.

I hover, lingering in the inversion and the afterglow of the moment, and then I flutter my wings too, trying to rise to meet her but I cannot. My wings are heavy, like lead. They feel cold. So, so cold. And then they catch fire, turning to gray ash with a rush of bright red, like a wave of embers. Then my wings are gone, and I am falling.

Falling. Falling.

Falling into endless gray.

When I hit the hard, rocky surface of the planet, I explode into a million meaningless pieces.

I awoke to a world of pain and cold. There was the steady hiss of gas escaping, and my lungs felt like they were full of liquid, but the roar of the sonic storm was gone, receded into background.

Against the grip of ice forming on my eyelids, I opened my eyes. I was upside down, still strapped into my chair, surrounded by wreckage and smoke. The curve of the vessel's lower sphere had refused to yield to the force of the storm—my design had held there at least. But the rim of the connecting pipe had cracked. That was where the hiss was coming from. Already there was frost forming on the walls. It would not be long before we lost all our air and warmth.

I blinked rapidly and unstrapped myself from the chair, falling onto the top dome of the lower sphere. That motion disturbed the unstable equilibrium of the vessel enough for it to tumble over and fall on its side. I lost my balance and fell too, into Njeriri. Her knee dug into my back, and I cried out. She didn't react. I picked myself up and saw her head hanging limply at an unnatural position like a damaged doll's. Her neck was broken. When I lifted her face, I saw that her eyes were empty, glassy things, already glittering white and crystalline with the first of growing frost. The hiss of the leak seemed to grow louder. And there was a new sound too. A buzzing in my ears. All around me, the windows showed nothing but the dead gray of the lower atmospheric haze we had fallen into, and the panels and consoles and viewscreens clicked and hummed erratically.

Ráxaxar screeched and groaned as he too slowly regained consciousness. There was a large, jagged piece of glass from one of the broken viewscreens poking out from his side, where the sensitive buds that ran from his hip to his underarm were. The shard looked like a strange barnacle growing between his outer scales. Thick black blood leaked out from the wound. It must have been incredibly painful. When he stood up out of the chair, he coughed out more thick blood.

"Are you okay?" I asked.

He gave me a single nod, lifted his index finger, and went to check on the vibrational panels. He was single-minded, that one.

"Gwaato! Can you hear me?" It was Beni-maru.

"Yes, I'm here," I said, turning to see him unstrap himself from his chair. He rolled out of it clumsily and stood up to face me. His face was scratched badly, and he favored his right leg as he came over.

"Ráxaxar?"

I cocked my head in the Aq'pa's direction. Beni-maru nodded.

"Njeriri?"

I shook my head and pointed at her corpse beside me.

"Shit." He cursed when he saw her. But there was no shock or sadness in his reaction. And then he said, "The hull is breached. We have to get into our atmospheric exposure suits," loud enough for Ráxaxar to hear.

The strain of breathing increasingly cold and dense air was a miserable weight in my chest. I stepped toward the side compartment of my console where we stored our suits, each one custom made to fit our anatomies. A last resort in case of worst-case scenario and we were indeed in the worst-case scenario. Or not far from it anyway.

As I slid my limbs into my suit, my face began to tingle where metal met flesh. I touched a hand to the metal half of my face, and it was like touching a block of smooth ice. Cold. Too cold. With a leak in the inner hull, there was a next-to-nil chance we would make it back up to Mogi-ku. And without Njeriri, the *next-to* was tending asymptotically closer to that *nil*. The vessel was designed to withstand external pressure and impact, but not to lift with an internal rupture. We would never be able to gain enough buoyancy in that condition.

Tears ran warm onto my cheeks before turning to ice. Crystal frustrations. I looked down, trying to hide the tears from Beni-maru and Ráxaxar who had already donned their bulky custom suits and connected their air tanks and radios.

"Can you stop the leak?" Beni-maru asked, voice muffled through the bulky helmet.

Pulling my suit up to my torso, I said, "I can try to use the sealant. But it's not even half as strong as the no'orin composites."

"Will it hold, though?" He seemed preternaturally calm. Emotionless almost, like he was mentally checking items off a checklist and not facing the prospect of death.

"No." I shook my head. "But it could keep us alive a bit longer. Give us more time."

"I see," Beni-maru said.

With the words said out loud, realization settled on me like a heavy cloak. We were all going to die. A wave of nausea hit, and I felt lightheaded for a moment as bile surged up my throat. We had fallen farther into the harsh atmosphere of the planet than anyone else ever had, and we would never live to tell the tale. Perhaps no one would ever find out. Ochoyo-Tananari would probably cover up this failed expedition and take the financial hit. Maybe use the catalytic polymer compositing process I developed to make herself a nice profit or improve upon it and try again later with some other smart and desperate fool seeking ii-mo in the treacherous depths of the world.

"Then it is as The Mother wills it. We move to the backup plan for returning to Moki-gu. Get your suit on. We will go outside and test the vibrational panels." Beni-maru indicated the door with a jut of his jaw.

"The panels? Now?" I asked, confused. I hadn't even known there was a backup plan for returning to the city that could work without Njeriri. "We should be focused on figuring out a way to survive and get back home."

"Right now, those panels are our only chance. They *are* the backup plan," he said firmly. And then he added, pointing to the waiting Aq'pa. "Ráxaxar is a conductive."

My eyes went wide as it all suddenly made sense.

Ráxaxar was a conductive. Of course. One of the Iji-omoji. One of the children of the storm, whose internal frequency could align to the natural frequency of some sonic storms. Resonate. Survive direct exposure to the weaker storms and even channel some of a storm's power directly to Ririni crystals without destroying themselves. They'd used those abilities to manually mine sonic storms near the meridian long before the vibration panels had been invented. But they could only do that with smaller storms up above. But down here, below the yedede'kiyan the storms did not discriminate. Their sonic frequency may have been the same as the storms, but the storm's amplitude was too thunderous to be contained or channeled by any living person. Iji-omoiji or not.

I had overheard researchers in the Kin-Ochoyo facility speculating on what would happen if an Iji-omoiji used their ability to help control and amplify the absorption potential of the new Kin-Ochoyo panels while they were channeling the storms. Something would happen, but what? Would there be constructive or destructive interference?

"That is the main reason he is here," Beni-maru admitted. "To help us execute the backup plan. We test the panels. If they work, we will attempt to use some of the energy absorbed from a supermassive storm to trigger a launch and send ourselves back up to Mogi-ku. Ráxaxar will try to control the release of energy to stabilize the ascent as much as possible."

I understood then why Beni-maru and Ochoyo-Tananari had kept their backup plan from me. Perhaps it was in part because they did not want me to know they were even considering the possibility that the vessel would fail but it was also because this backup plan was not a plan at all, it was madness. An uncontrolled launch in a compromised vessel under manual control by an Iji-omoiji? I shook my head at the thought. It would be a rough ascent at best, and the chance of it working was slim. But then, I considered that at least it did what all good backup plans did—it gave us a chance. And if Ráxaxar truly was an Iji-omoiji, perhaps that chance was further away from zero than I had thought.

Besides, we had no other options. And very little time.

I nodded and hurried to catch up, sliding my arms awkwardly into the stiff suit and pulling the helmet up and over my head. The echo of my own thoughts and the smell of my own breath, ripe with rising bile filled my head. My body was a collection of aches where the suit pressed against my flesh. I activated the life support system and felt the vacuum hiss of the suit sealing. Lights flashed messages on the front of my visor, the voice of the onboard computer began to reel off data. Battery power, pressure, temperature, all the basics that let me know I was still alive. Suddenly, a red blinking light appeared in the lower left corner of my visor and flickered there. The onboard computer began to insistently warn me that the mounted heat exchanger on the back of my suit was malfunctioning.

"Shit."

I requested additional diagnostics, and the computer sang out a string of numbers.

It was the controller on the heat pump that had failed. When we crashed, the suit had come loose from the storage area brace and must have hit something hard enough to scramble the internal electronics. It would take hours to repair or try to replace it with the one from Njeriri's. There wasn't nearly enough time.

I choked back a sob.

Without the heat exchanger on my suit, I was doomed. It would last a few minutes at best, but it could only slow my death, not protect me from it.

"Gwaato! Hurry up," Beni-maru called to me.

"Yes," I shouted back, my voice rising to a whine. "Yes."

The falling tears turned to rivulets.

It was cruel.

To have come so far, so close to what I had dreamed of for many juzu only to die before I could witness it with my own eyes because of a badly stored suit. I tried to blink the tears away, angry at the humiliation of weeping but even more angry at the stupidity of the manner in which my death would arrive. Not from the storm, or the crash, but from fucking equipment failure. I didn't want to die, and certainly not like that.

I wiped the tears with the back of my hand.

"What in The Mother's blessed silence is taking you so long, Gwaato? We need to get going," Beni-maru said, helping Ráxaxar awkwardly carry the box of panels toward the door. The emergency repair kit was attached to the arm of his suit.

My damaged suit would not last long outside. Ten to fifteen minutes at best. But wearing the suit inside the vessel would slow down the freezing and give me more time, perhaps an hour. Not much more, but perhaps that was all I could hope for.

"Hey Beni-maru, can I stay inside?" I asked.

"What?"

"Can I stay here, inside the vessel?"

I didn't say why because I didn't want him to know my suit was damaged. "Do you really need me outside to test the panels?"

"No." He seemed irritated by the question. "I need you to help me rig the Ririni crystals to the base of the vessel for thrust. Staying in here will achieve nothing except dying slower, so whatever is making you hesitate, get over it and get your suit on. We don't have time!"

All the care in his voice was gone, replaced by something colder and more calculating. He didn't sound like the man I had come to think of as a friend. He seemed to notice it too.

"I'm sorry, Gwaato. I didn't mean it like that. But please, we need to hurry."

I remembered what Njeriri said about him and decided it was better to be seen as a coward than a liability.

"Sure," I replied.

I finished my suit checks and turned on the radio, my mind still racing, trying to figure out another way to survive. I couldn't die. Not after coming so far. Not while the chance to get back to Moki-gu existed. Not while we still had a plan B, however unlikely it was. I had to find a way to get back up and hear my mother tell me the words I had dreamt of—that she was wrong, and I was right all along. Or at the very least, see the acknowledgement in her eyes even if she couldn't form the words.

The steady whoosh of escaping air and the beeping of the heat exchanger warning reminded me that my time was limited. There was a clock attached to my life.

"Ready," I said over the radio.

Beni-maru grunted and pressed the panel to open the lower sphere door as he and Ráxaxar carried the box of panels out. The vessel sat on its side, so it slid open to the right, revealing a strange, murky white-and-gray world.

I could barely see more than a meter ahead. I turned up the gain on my helmet visor and blinked rapidly as my eyes adjusted. We were on a slope, the side of one of the mountain continents. I could hear the roar of methane geysers and erupting lava all around us, but I could not see where they were coming from. The rocks near us were not the pure black of those in the inversion layer, but interbedded with layers of rich reds and whites and yellows that reminded me of the Ochoyo tribal band pattern on the Tanti'ti shack. Ice had corticated on the surface of our fallen vessel like hyaline moss.

When I saw the warped structure of the damaged connecting pipe from outside, I finally knew what had doomed us. Thermal fatigue. I hadn't accounted for the effect of a reversal in thermal stresses and strains due to rapid temperature changes from cold to hot and back again. The material strength of my polymers was hysteric in nature, but no one, certainly not me, had expected a thermal inversion layer in the atmosphere, especially not one hot enough to warm the atmospheric gases above critical conditions. The temperature reversal had weakened the polymer mechanical strength enough for the storm to do its damage.

I shook my head. I was so sure I had thought of everything. Considered every possibility. I was wrong.

"We need to get close to a storm without getting killed," Beni-maru said over the radio, pulling my attention back to the moment and the fact of the horrible fate barreling down on me. He and Ráxaxar set the black box down on the ground and looked around, adjusting their helmets.

Beni-maru pointed east. "I think I see a flash of light. Ráxaxar, can you carry the panels a few kilometers in that direction by yourself while we stabilize the vessel and rig it for launch?"

The Aq'pa signed something that I assumed meant that he could, the articulated joints of his suit making him appear clumsy.

Only an Iji-omoiji would willingly walk in the direction of a sonic storm.

"Good," Beni-maru said. "Be careful, and don't get too close. The storms here aren't like the ones you're used to."

I could already feel my breath getting cold, the damaged heat exchanger meant that I would soon be breathing air with the consistency of glassy slush.

It took all the will I had to not just sit on the cold, rocky ground and cry from fear, waiting to die.

Ráxaxar awkwardly lugged his load, moving into the distance until he was out of sight, his form swallowed by the white and gray haze. I could still hear his laboured breathing on the open radio channel.

Beni-maru pointed to the fallen upper sphere. "Quickly, I'll inspect the vessel. Patch it up enough that its integrity will survive an uncontrolled launch. You can start opening the base of the vessel where we will position the Ririni crystals."

"Okay."

He moved toward the vessel and grabbed onto a strut, inspecting the vents. And then he turned on the friction pads of his suit and climbed the bottom bulb of the vessel, up to the connecting pipe. He seemed completely uninterested in observing the environment around us, in witnessing the wonder of what had never been witnessed before.

I walked past him, taking in as much of it as I could. All the ii-mo. There was so much I wanted to gather. Geological, electromagnetic, biological, all kinds of new and wonderful data. But the rising cold in my lungs kept drawing my focus back to survival. I had only a few minutes before I'd start to die. But what else could I have done except go along with his plan?

I was about to start opening the reinforced base of the vessel which supported the weight of the control chamber we'd been cocooned in, when I heard a loud hiss, a thud and then a cry. It was Beni-maru.

I got up and ran over to the side of the vessel to see him sprawled out on the ground, unconscious. If Ráxaxar had heard the fall, he didn't react to it. The open channel stayed quiet.

I switched to Beni-maru's private channel. "Beni-maru!"

Had he slipped and fallen? Had the residual gas vented and thrown him off? I didn't know, but he wasn't responding.

Seeing him there like that, so still and unmoving, the solution to a horrible calculus resolved itself in my mind. Beni-maru was close enough to my size that I could fit in his suit.

I choked back nausea at the thought, but the insistent beep of the failing heat exchanger did not allow me to let go of the evil thought.

I knelt by his side and inspected him. His suit looked undamaged by the fall, and I looked through his visor. He'd probably just landed in a bad position and temporarily lost consciousness. It looked like he was still breathing. My own icy breath drove desperation deeper into my mind with each lungful.

Before I could stop myself, I yanked on the two emergency release cables to open his helmet. The polymer joiners unlatched with a snap and a hiss. I gasped.

He didn't move at first and so I thought that he'd truly died from the fall but then his eyes shot open, and his mouth opened wide, a scream frozen in his throat.

"I'm sorry," I muttered as I scrambled away from him on my haunches, taking his helmet with me. He grabbed at his neck, his body trying to process the viscous, cold, and dense air but he was drowning. His limbs thrashed and spasmed. Wide, his freezing eyes fixed on me with glassy accusation.

I turned away, struggling to keep my stomach from spilling out its contents.

"I'm sorry, Beni-maru," I whispered, shaking my head. "I'm so sorry."

Once I was sure he was dead, I put his helmet back on his head, grabbed his legs and pulled him back inside the vessel. I waited a few tense seconds for the hiss of the door to vent most of the heavy unbreathable air that had followed me in and bring the temperature back to survivable levels. Then I pulled Beni-maru's suit off, taking care not to look at those vitrified eyes. But the feel of his cold lifeless hands reminded me of the time, so long ago when they had held mine as I waited for my mother to return from one of her travels. I could not hold back the tears, but I could not stop what I was doing either. I did not want to die.

The persistent hiss of the hull leak followed me through every action, every thud of limbs falling, and latch undoing was loud against the background noise of gargling and sighing and buzzing of malfunctioning pumps, electrical systems, and filters that were desperately trying to the keep the breached chamber endurable. But my sobs echoed back to me loudest of all.

I fumbled Beni-maru's body into my own damaged suit and sealed the helmet so that Ráxaxar would not know what I had done when he returned. And then I got into Beni-maru's suit. The fit was a bit tight around the midsection, he was thinner than I was. I sucked in my stomach and pulled the suit up. It was good enough to seal. I wiped away my tears and donned the helmet, reactivating the suit. The vital signs monitoring came online, a steady vibration of information to my cochlea. The radio light came on too, sound crackling quietly into my ear.

I exhaled relief and inhaled fresh guilt.

It was all my fault. Njeriri was dead because I had overlooked a calculation of thermal hysteresis. Beni-maru was dead because I was not brave enough to bear the weight of my own failure and accept the fate I had been dealt.

A wave of light-headedness came over me and I took a moment to let it pass. Three quick shallow breaths, one especially long and deep and then I was ready to go out again. It wasn't over. I'd just bought myself more time. We still had to launch the vessel.

Back outside, the wind had picked up and was roaring despite the noise isolation of my helmet. Tiny carbon dioxide crystals clinked against my suit. The visibility had reduced to nearly nothing and the visor gain couldn't compensate enough for it. The world was all rock and ice and wind and the broken vessel next to me which meant either Ráxaxar had found a nearby sonic storm to test the panels with or a sonic storm had found me, and I was going to die anyway.

I activated the suit's friction pads and carefully climbed the bottom bulb of the vessel, up to the connecting pipe, as Beni-maru had done. I could see where the material had warped with the rapid temperature changes. A swelling of the polymer like a skin inflammation. And at the junction, the tiny fissure that had doomed us.

I detached the emergency repair kit from the arm of the suit and was about to start applying the special polymer sealant when I heard Ráxaxar's clicking and bellowing explode into the radio. It was a low guttural sound that made my skin crawl, but it was impossible to miss the absolute terror it carried.

Something was wrong.

I looked up from the fissure. Three luminescent balls dancing with electric blue fire appeared from the hazy atmosphere like angry ghosts. They slammed into me with an explosion that was so loud, it drowned out the transmission of Ráxaxar's agony and the sound of my own scream. It blotted out every other sound except my own heartbeat. I felt the crackle of lightning surge through me as the world tilted at an angle—steep.

As I fell, I saw more orbs of bright azure lightning sweep by like bizarre electric hail. I had never seen or heard of anything like it before. Was this too a previously unrecorded phenomenon? For a moment, falling through the haze, a flash of the excitement of discovery shot to my head. And then I crashed back to the reality of the situation, hard. Hit the rocky ground with a sickening crack. For a moment, I feared that the helmet was broken, and I remember thinking that The Mother, in her divine irony, was going to do to me what I had done to Beni-maru, but I was surprised to find that I didn't die.

I scrambled to my feet and crawled to the door of the vessel, crunching dry ice and rock underfoot. Another sonic storm. But I knew that even with compromised structural integrity, the no'orin polymer of the vessel was still my best chance of survival.

Long chains of lightning tore down from above, explosively digging into the ground all around me like the planet itself was setting down pillars of pure energy to claim its domain.

I dived inside the vessel just as an impossibly loud guttural sound blotted out my senses. Darkness fell like a curtain and my feet were lifted off the ground. I vibrated violently, like every cell in my body had been set to some powerful sonic frequency. I lost all sense of direction, of time, of everything. I know I was screaming but the sound was the world, and I was nothing but a whisper within it.

I don't know how long it lasted. Or what happened to me while it did. But when it was over, and the edges of reality became clear and well-defined again, I opened my eyes and saw chaos.

The vessel was intact, but barely so. Cracks ran all along the sphere like it was an egg, radiating out from the fissure I had tried to seal. The windows were cracked and all the viewscreens next to the panels were broken. Njeriri and Beni-maru's bodies had been flung to opposing sides, their limbs at acute, impossible angles. And yet, I was still alive, unharmed except for a terrible pain in my left shoulder.

The altimeter of Njeriri's pilot panel was still beeping out our depth. Seventy-eight kilometers below the meridian. We'd fallen far. Perhaps my mother had been right after all. Perhaps there was no surface. I walked on wobbly legs to the door and opened it.

I entered a ribbon of pure white haze. Beneath, I felt the ground still sloping down. Wherever the sonic storm had dumped the vessel, I was still on the mountain continent's edge. I walked forward, gingerly taking steps, unable to tell what lay ahead of me. I wondered briefly if I could find Ráxaxar in this shrouded, desolate landscape. If the Aq'pa was still alive. Perhaps the sonic storm had shown mercy to him, being an Iji-omoji.

I'd only gone a few meters when my suit picked up a tremor. The ground shivered and there was a rumbling in the distance just ahead. Something could have been happening right in front of me and I couldn't see it through the haze. The terror of unknowing seized me and I rooted myself in place, trying to decide if I should run back to the broken vessel or press ahead. Suddenly, the ground beneath me gave and began to move, solid rock and ice flowing fitfully and unevenly, like some strange porridge.

"No. No. No," I repeated as I fell on my hands and knees. By the time it was close enough to see, it was too late. An avalanche of scree and ice, glittering and glinting bright against the sea of white.

I shouted as I was swept away, sliding atop the moving slice of ground that had given up its grip on the mountain continent. The sensor alarms of my stolen suit were a riot of warnings I could not heed.

Was this some tectonic after-effect of the sonic storm? I wondered as fear gripped me again. It was becoming a familiar sensation. This part of the planet was a wild creature made of rocky fangs and icy claws: the temperature and the pressure and the ball lightning and the thermal inversion and the methane geysers and the lava and the starlike floods of ice and rock that mocked the very concept of survival.

Our kind was not meant to be here.

I hugged myself as I slid down. Then there was a lurch, and I was flung up and off the edge of the slope. A cliff. Flailing, I reached out, hoping my fingers would find purchase on something, anything before I fell and scattered on jagged rock below.

My heart leapt when I felt the fingers of the suit dig into rock. I activated the friction pads and dug into the vertical edge of hard icy rock. Flattened myself to the cliff wall, feeling for better handholds and footholds as I thanked The Mother that I could not see how far the fall was. Ice and rock spray rained down on me, but I bent my head down and held on and waited.

When it stopped, I hauled myself up, one hand at a time, over the lip of the ledge, breathing heavily. I lay there, for a moment, eyes closed, gasping.

The weight of everything that had happened settled on me. The mélange of emotions thundering their way through my mind crashed against each other. I felt too much. It was too much.

I started to laugh. It was a strange laugh, a foreign sound, even to me. I laughed for a while and then I screamed and then I started to cry because I realized that Ráxaxar could not have survived the storm or the avalanche without the vessel which meant he was dead and so that meant I would soon be dead too. There was no more plan B. Despite what I had done, death was inexorable, like gravity.

I rose to my feet. There was no way to climb back up. It would take weeks and the suits were not designed to survive more than a dozen hours or so. There was nothing left to do but continue for as long as Beni-maru's suit would take me. Continue to descend until I found the bottom of the mountain-continent and fell off, drowning in supercritical atmosphere, or I reached the solid surface my mother said didn't exist. The best I could hope for was that I would finally find ii-mo, true knowledge before I found death. If the planet was so determined to kill me, then I would trade it my life for its secrets. I continued my slow walk downslope, one step at a time, feeling my way down the rough terrain.

So here I am.

I have been climbing my way down the frigid rock slope for more than eight hours without incident and I am yet to reach the end of the world, but my battery is finally giving out.

The sensor in the suit reads more than thirty times the normal atmospheric pressure near the meridian and the temperature is negative hundred but the heat exchanger still seems to be running at a normal efficiency. Oxygen pressure is lower than it should be, but that's to be expected with the low battery.

I cannot go back up, go back home, so I must continue to go down, pulled by an emotional alloy of curiosity and guilt like an anchor—three are dead, one by my own hand. It has to be worth something, some knowledge of what lies below. It has to.

I keep moving along the slope, until unexpectedly, my feet sink into what feels like a puddle of water. Beneath, the ground is flat and smooth, nothing like the craggy edge of the mountain-continent. I look down. I can barely see so I ramp up the heat exchanger and vent some of the warm air. Burn precious battery. The temperature goes up with a whirr and some of the hazy atmosphere in front of me clears away like a ghost retreating to rest with the ancestors in Eh'waizo. I can see the silver liquid comes up to about the height of my ankles and runs as far as I can see, which is only two meters or so. I take a few more careful steps forward and it's the same. I'm walking through a kind of shallow silver lake. I take in a long breath, struck by the possibility that the planet has a shallow water body or even an ocean, a thin rim of liquid running all along its surface. Its smooth, crystalline surface.

Great Mother.

Signs of a surface. I should feel elated. But I feel nothing but a hollow sadness and resignation.

I step forward, sinking deeper into the silver water and into a sudden, perfect silence. I can see the concentric silver ripples spread out where my body makes contact, but I hear nothing, so I turn up the external audio receptors of the suit. Still, nothing. Not even the whirr of the heat exchanger. Or the rush of wind. Absolute silence. When I take a step back, sound returns to the world.

I know what it is then.

The maadiregi at the temple of the talking drum call them The Silences. Naturally occurring bubbles of soundlessness where nothing vibrates even at the subatomic level, except living creatures animated by the Mothersound. Pockets of divine quiet, the antithesis of the sonic storms. Considered holy sites for communion with The Mother, to hear her more clearly. The maadiregi that visit The Silences sometimes sit there, stripped of their magical abilities, waiting upon her revelations.

I am amazed to find one here, so far down, sitting atop a shallow silver ocean.

I step forward, again into The Silence.

The hush returns. Soul-deep and soothing. I let out a yell, but I cannot hear myself, only feel the stretching of my face and neck muscles, the tension in my jaw, the strain on my tongue. I walk forward, wading through the silver ocean, deeper into The Silence, relishing the preternatural quiet.

As I progress, a chill seizes my bones and I start to shiver as though the cold air has finally found a leak in my suit to thread its way into. I cannot hear any sensor warnings, but instinctively, as though The

Mother has told me herself, I know I am not shivering because of a leak. I am shivering with awe at this vast and terrible and wonderful and strange world.

I press on until I take a step and feel myself float up, suspended for a moment, before dropping down again. Just above the interface between the silver liquid and the supercritical fluid above, the atmosphere is so dense that I can almost swim in it.

Floating in The Silence is freeing. I do it again, leaping higher and floating longer this time. I reach up into the misty world with the bulky arm of the atmospheric exposure suit. The supercooled atmospheric molecules that are balanced on some thermodynamic tightrope I don't fully understand turn to crystals at my touch, like magic. I gasp noiselessly.

I am in a daydream at the bottom of the world where the natural magic and physics of the world have conspired to birth something impossible. A place where I can hardly see in front of me, where gas and liquid are undifferentiable twins and crystals bloom from the air at the slightest touch, where bubbles of silence swell like The Mother herself has hushed the world as bursts of incredible sonic energy appear at random in tantrums, wild and untamed.

I am overwhelmed and exhausted. I sink to my knees in the silver liquid. I close my eyes and take in a deep breath.

And then I hear it.

I brought you here to see this.

The voice enters my mind with a force I am not expecting, breaking the silence like glass. It sounds like my mother's voice but with an infinite chorus. Like every word she says is repeated by every woman who was and is and is to come.

I wonder briefly if I am losing my mind.

It is time for my children to know more of their world. You have fulfilled your purpose. Those that come after you will find what remains and know that you succeeded. That you were the first to descend.

I open my eyes but there is no one and nothing but white and silver in the hazy landscape.

"Are you . . . ?" I ask, not daring to speak her name.

Yes.

Another shiver streaks through me.

"Can you save me?" I whisper into the silence as a surge of hope swells in my heart. "Can you tell me the word for flight so I can return home, to my mother?"

No.

"Please," I beg.

No. You cannot return. You owe a life.

The shivers turn to a persistent tremble.

There is a balance. An accounting. Between every word, there is a pause. For every action, there is a reaction. Life and death. The light and the dark. The sound and the silence. The known and the uncertain. There is a balance.

My head falls and I remain quiet for a while. And then, "Will my mother ever know?" I ask. "Will she know that I was the first to reach the surface?"

Yes. And it will not matter. You sought to see below the yedede'kiyan and now that you have, you have only found more mysteries. You seek to know what causes my sonic storms? What causes the thermal inversion? What creates The Silences? What animates your reality and what unfolds at the edges of the universe? Then seek. You will find answers, but at the end of every answer, there will always be another question. There is a balance. The boundary condition of all knowledge is faith.

I blink at that. Those are the last words my mother said to me. Maybe I am imagining all this. Maybe there really is a leak in my suit, and I cannot tell so my mind is succumbing to hypothermia. Maybe I am having a conversation with myself as I die.

My creation is unknowable in its fullness. It is to be experienced. Not analyzed, not controlled, not fully understood. I have let you experience this world and allowed you as much understanding as you deserve. Now, pay the cost of what I have given.

It all makes a kind of bitter sense in my mind, so I say, "I accept. I will pay."

There is a glow ahead, like diffuse light streaming through the haze.

Walk.

I rise to my feet and continue to press forward toward the light, wading deeper and deeper into The Silence until I emerge from the other side.

Sound returns and I hear the splash of silver liquid beneath, the rush of wind whooshing by and the steady beeping of all my atmospheric exposure suit alarms. The battery has failed.

Return the sound that animates you.

Suddenly, the atmosphere hisses and there is a sound like the end of the world that sets my head pounding with deep reverberations. A blast of pressure hits my suit, and the oxygen valve screams open to compensate, but not quickly enough. My ears ring and my sinuses ache.

The sonic storm appears in front of me like a beast in all its bright blue rage and wild glory. Gigantic tendrils of lightning vein out of the haze like a spreading infection, so large it seems they are moving in slow motion. My breath turns to ice, and I clutch at my chest as the heat exchanger and all the other life support equipment connected to the battery finally, completely, give out.

As I am swallowed by the sound and the surge of energy scatters me like a dried out, brittle husk, I finally accept it. I accept it all. I accept my death and I pray for entry into Eh'waizo. I accept that nothing is certain. That nothing is clear. That faith and knowledge are inseparable. That The Mother has created us for both joy and suffering. That life and death are two sides of the same thing. That I am a pioneer. That I am a follower. That I am an orphan, and I am my mother's son. That I am a murderer. That I am human. That I love my mother even though I hate her deeply. That the search for knowledge is endless and futile but necessary. That there is a balance and a price to all things, even knowledge. Especially knowledge. That, in the end, we must all learn to both conquer and submit to Órino-Rin, this strange and lovely and terrible world of sound and fury that both nurtures and destroys us, like an inconstant mother.

ABOUT THE AUTHOR

Wole Talabi is an engineer, writer, and editor from Nigeria. He is the author of the World Fantasy award nominated novel *Shigidi and the Brass Head of Obalufon* (DAW books/Gollancz) one of the *Washington Posts* Top Ten Science fiction and fantasy books of 2023 which was also nominated for the Nebula, Locus, and British Fantasy awards. His short fiction has appeared in places like *Asimov's Science Fiction, Lightspeed Magazine, Africa Risen,* and is collected in the books *Convergence Problems* (DAW books, 2024) and *Incomplete Solutions* (Luna Press, 2019). He has also been a finalist for the Hugo, BSFA, and Crawford awards, as well as the Caine Prize for African Writing. He won the Nommo award for African speculative fiction and the Sidewise award for Alternate History. He has edited five anthologies including the acclaimed *Africanfuturism: An Anthology* (Brittlepaper, 2020) and *Mothersound: The Saoútiverse Anthology* (Android Press, 2023). He likes scuba diving, elegant equations, and oddly shaped things. He currently lives and works in Australia.

Oh Time Thy Pyramids

ANN LEBLANC

My mother was born into perfect stillness, and abides in laudatory silence to this day. As a child, I spent centuries at her side, and at no point did I ever see her shift the barest fraction of her body. No movement, neither intended nor involuntary, ever marred her voiceless song.

I think my mother has never forgiven me for the first time I smiled.

Like all children, I was a promise of the triumph of death over life, and like all good children, I stood at her side, silent and still, from the moment of my creation until the moment of my death.

The song is the first thing I remember. I was born-awoken in one of the smaller chambers of the universal tomb, and the song echoed from one end to the other, chanted notes rising to the ornate vaulted ceiling, dancing between the volcanic glass buttresses, and curling round the piled treasures of the Perfected Conquest.

The room of my birth was dedicated to memorializing the woodworking trade of a planet that never existed, but had nevertheless been perfectly conquered. I spent my childhood standing perfectly still, singing to a collection of bandsaws, drill presses, chisels, hand planes, and other silent tools. None of them had ever been used, or even plugged in. The universe had already been conquered and the tomb had already been built, so there was no need to create anything new.

My mother never spoke a single word to me. Her song was to be my comfort and my education. My body was designed to resonate with her words until I could harmonize independently.

The first thing I learned was that the Queen had created the universe after she died, and she died before she conquered both the universe and Death. All things in the universe belong to the Queen and her conquest. All peoples and all objects are hers and hers alone. The universe will end when the song is perfect and the Queen will step backwards into life, again to conquer and then create the universe.

The hard facts of the song are surely familiar to you, but it is important that I establish my bonafides before I break them on the shoals of your silence. Like the song, some stanzas must by necessity be sung before others for harmony to occur.

I sang and I sang and I sang. Endless centuries passed and I was content. Not happy, not joyous, not loved, but content. The woodworking room and the song were all I knew, and the song was infinite so there were always new phrases to learn, new aspects of the Perfected Conquest to understand.

My first crime was boredom.

I didn't even realize the song was repeating itself until I was a decade past the loop-point. Then, two years of mounting dread at the familiarity of each word and phrase. A single moment can last a century, and it took a century before I was sure.

Shame quickly followed boredom.

My purpose was to sing the song, to love the Queen, to hope she would heal from the fractal-fatal wounds that poisoned her perfect star-sized mind. Any dissatisfaction with this task was a flaw in my soul. Better to die than allow myself to be bored. In each of the numberless chambers of the universe there are an infinite number of peoples who represent each and every one of the possible persons who could've been conquered by the Queen. In all the time the universe had existed, none of them had ever deviated from the perfection of the song—according to the song.

What was wrong with me, that I could feel this way? The words of praise rotted in my mouth, and I didn't care anymore if the Queen lived or died or even failed in her constructive conquest.

Fear followed shame.

I was flawed, and so surely one of the infinite followers of the Queen would arrive to denounce me. Or surely my own mother would chastise me. Another five centuries I waited, my boredom and shame and fear growing and growing, wrapping my heart like an invasive vine.

Nothing. Nothing. Nothing. Just the stillness and the song, forever and ever. I detected no deviations in the song. If the song contained *everything*, then why didn't it mention my crime? Perhaps I had only escaped scrutiny by containing my crime to my thoughts. Maybe if I remained perfectly still for the rest of time, I would be allowed to think whatever I wanted.

• • •

A mere century passed before my second crime.

How corrupt I was to fall so far in such a short time! I wanted to know what movement felt like, and it only took a century before I gave in. My second crime was to allow my left-upper index finger to twitch a single millimeter.

The memory of that millimeter remains as powerful now as it was in the moment. I was simultaneously bowled over by both the horror of my infraction and the ecstasy of action.

My third crime followed immediately. I smiled.

I couldn't help it! I had moved, and remained alive. I had experienced true pleasure for the first time in my life, and the song remained unchanged. I was damned by my crime, and I remained damned, and so my fourth, fifth, sixth, and seventh crimes all followed immediately, like I was a satellite tumbling down an inescapable gravity well.

For all my life, I had been still. For eons, my vision had been fixed upon a green-enameled bandsaw. I had contemplated the flexible curve of the blade, the well-considered shape of the metal housing, its stolid weight and color, the way it—like me—was capable of motion, but remained perfectly still. It had occupied my vision for so long that in my mind's eye I no longer perceived it.

I had never seen my mother's face.

I resolved to turn my head towards the sound of her voice, but the motion sickened me. How terrible to learn that the universe was not fixed, that through something as small as my will alone, I could move the firmament. My vision blurred, my body buzzed and churned, sickened at the absence of my companion the bandsaw. And then I saw her.

I had sung of beauty. I had sung of love.

I saw neither of these virtues in my mother's face, but rather something deeper and truer than my loyalty to the Queen. My mother's intricately braided hair, the scintillation of light in her compound eyes, and her coral-colored exoskeleton, flawless from head to alitrunk to petiole to gaster, were full of subtleties more sublime than I had ever imagined.

In an instant, I was transfixed. The flaw that had caused my crimes wasn't internal to me, but the universe itself, for having placed me such that I could not see my mother.

Even during the worst moments of my doubt, I had never stopped singing the song of the perfected conquest. With the problem of my gaze solved, I regained all the passion I had lost for the song, and then some more. No longer was I singing to the Queen, but to my own mother. When I sang of the great deeds of the Queen, I imagined I was singing about my mother instead. I did not care that it was heresy, because I already knew that I would not be punished for the secret horrors hidden in my own heart.

I sang this way for seventy thousand years.

Doubt gnawed at the melody for five hundred thousand years.

Even as I stared transfixed at my mother, my mother did not look at me. Her many lenses were cast upwards in adulation, as if the Queen herself hovered in the air above us. Not only had my mother not turned to look at me during the brief occurrence of my initial crimes, but she had not rebuked me in any way. Her song had never wavered, her body had never moved. At first, I believed this as her modeling perfection so that I might emulate her; then I came to understand the lack of response was a rebuke in and of itself.

After several millennia, desperation took hold. The idea that my mother had not noticed my crimes brought no relief. What did it mean to believe my mother loved me, if that love had never been tested?

I wanted so badly to love her—to love anything—but love was not enough. Love had been ground to dust by the weight of millennia. And I who had stood nearly-still for all that time had nothing to fill the emptiness that love's absence left behind.

It took me an entire year to realize I had stopped singing. The song still resounded in the room, even if my voice no longer joined the chorus. For an entire year, I had committed an unthinkable crime, and not even noticed.

And nothing had happened.

Nothing. Nothing. Nothing. No sight but my mother's face, frozen in adulation. No sound but her song, deafened by my own silence. And so I twitched my finger again. The gulf between no crimes and one crime is far vaster than one crime and two crimes. With each infraction, the weight of my sin grew heavier, but the activation energy required for the next one decreased.

It wasn't long before I attempted to walk. I had seen within the song the manner in which a person walks, and yet the reality of coordinating a body was beyond me. I flopped on the ground, like a fish; unsteady like a newborn deer. I knew of such creatures, but to be one was like all the stanzas of the song collapsed into a single glorious note that went on and on and on.

Flopping became standing; standing became walking; walking became running. Movement was a sin; movement was a gift. I scampered from one end of my chamber to the other. Then began again, slower, carefully gazing at each tool, each frozen member of the chorus. The

Queen's tomb was infinite, and I found a bounded infinity of interest within that single room.

And when I had explored and contemplated every aspect of that room, I considered at last the problem of the doors. There were six of them. One on each of the six walls. I chose the door nearest to my mother, both to honor her, and to spite her. As I turned the wheel to unlock the door, as I pushed the ancient metal that was never meant to move, I waited—and hoped!—for my mother to finally react. To call me back, to grab me, to damn herself to save me. Nothing.

Thus began the era of my explorations and collections.

The second room was nearly a clone of my birth-room. More woodworking equipment, more funereal statues singing an endless song. My disappointment was so vast that I spent barely a year there.

The next room presented the same problem. And the next, and the next and so on. After less than a decade I was running—running!—through each room, choosing doors at random, giving each barely a glance, hoping to find something different, something new.

For the second time in my life, I understood the terrible problem of infinity. The Queen's tomb was the universe itself, spanning more than a million light years. I could run for a span of time that would dwarf my own lifespan, and still not escape the curse of familiarity. Slight variations on a theme were not enough. I needed more.

Without any guilt at all, I defiled the tomb itself. I peeled back the skin of the onion. I cut into the flesh of my prison, and held its guts gently in my multifold hands. My sin did not stay within me, but spread to the exoskeleton of the Queen's infinite repose.

And from the auguries of the tomb's wires and conduits, I learned to transform myself into a thought, to transmit myself to distant layers and rooms. Through my will I made infinity smaller.

For a time, I was happy to explore the tomb, and collect the very best of each category of object held within. I cleared rooms for my collections. I piled teacups made by artisans whose existence had been paved over by the conquest, but whose skill remained embodied in the things they made. I lay myself down on woven tapestries commemorating cultures whose only purpose within the Queen's cosmology was to be conquered.

But I never made anything myself.

The one constant of the eons of my roving sins was that all motion originated from my will alone. A painted nested figurine might topple from its perch, but only because I had set it there imperfectly. All else was still.

Until it wasn't.

I was sitting at the core of the region I named the Library of Ectopic Realities—whose words were written upon the ephemeral torn off wings of butterflies—when I heard a sound.

Footsteps.

Someone else's footsteps, clear as bells on the perfect parquet floors.

Before I could prepare myself, before I could even understand the importance of what I was hearing, I looked up from my book, and saw a woman.

A woman. Moving. Walking towards me, upright, stern-backed, with bright intent eyes, and lips full of determination. A terrible long-necked harpoon in her hands.

I screamed. I had never in all my millennia seen another person move. I had given up hope of ever not being alone. And none of the other funereal statues in the room moved to stop her, just as they had never moved to stop me.

I screamed so loud it burned away any other thought, charred to ash any possibility of fleeing or fighting. I would later learn that she couldn't hear my scream because without thinking I had screamed within the radio bands reserved for the song, and—though we would later argue about *why* that was the case—she was deaf to those frequencies.

When she greeted me, in a sonorous voice carried across the air with perfect diction, I believed I had already died. When she put the tip of her spear against the hard-shaggy exoskeleton between my eyes, I began to understand what death actually meant. I had sung of Death for eons—within the context of His defeat by the Queen—but because I had lived within eternity, I had not understood the mournful terror of He who the song called the Pale King. In that moment, I thought I understood, but I was wrong.

The woman spared me, and by sparing me, she doomed me.

Her name was Crisininimusticalion, and to her, I was nothing special. She told me that most people called her Crissy. Do you understand what I mean when I say most people? The tomb is infinite, and so it had been true arrogance to believe that I was the only one who had fallen from the Queen's song.

She shackled me with her voice, and pulled me along through silent light-hours to her home camp. Which was full of people who looked like her—bipedal with smooth and glistening skin—and people who looked like me—glorious exoskeleton containing a perfect segmented body.

But you must forgive me. My understanding of those first mere months when I became accustomed to living among others are a jumbled blur within my recollection. I had been accustomed to using the unhurried weight of centuries to accrete my memories. Slow slow slow, for all my life. And then I was around others who moved fast, talked fast. I was used to regarding a single object at a time, and now I was surrounded with multitudes who—in their hurry—talked over each other and whose voices did not harmonize like the chorus of the song, but created a cacophonous discord within my mind.

I could not look at the people for long, I could not listen to them. Instead I turned my focus to familiar ground and studied the tomb and the objects within it. Crissy and her people lived within a damaged region of the tomb. A great cataclysm had warped and twisted much of the hexagonal superstructure, and great tremors—which continued in lesser form during my stay there—had smashed every object upon the floor. Most rooms were too damaged to traverse—full of debris, including the pulverized remains of funereal statues like me.

It made sense to me then that so many people in this area had given up the song. I remember wishing that a similar cataclysm would occur within my own home region. I thought that such destruction might've even sown doubt within my perfect mother.

Eventually I became bored of the mundanity of destruction—entropy renders all things into soup—and tried harder to understand my heretical peers.

Crissy was my anchor amid the chaos of that time. She was so patient with me as I followed her everywhere, keeping her constantly in my vision like the green bandsaw had been my childhood constant. I was fascinated by the way she moved, like a dancer upon a plain of needle-sharp obelisks, forever falling towards death, yet forever fearless. Those two long legs kept her perfectly balanced against the obsessions and worries that weighed me down.

She was fierce too. A hunter like her people. I had not realized that the tomb was full of traps. They had never sprung for me, but the tomb considered her people to be anathema, and made itself a hostile place to them. And so they armored themselves in the shattered corpses of the tomb and its statues.

She was soft too. One day, I followed her into her tent after she returned from a salvaging expedition and watched as she removed her armor. Her secret skin matched the rich green color of her eyes.

Instinctively, I reached out to touch her with my fine manipulation arms, and she did not push me away with her voice, despite how vulnerable this made her. It shocked me how soft her skin was beneath my delicate lower hands. I understood intellectually where leather came from—having handled many fine leather goods—but the reality of skin was far stranger.

That night, she allowed me to sleep at the foot of her bed. In the morning, she called me her guard dog. I liked that, in part because I had included many taxidermied dogs within my collection. Later, she put a collar around my pronutum, which I liked even more, as a physical embodiment of the emotional leash that connected us.

That leash—having been made with corrupted hands in a corrupted place—long ago fell apart, dissolved by the unintentional cruelty of infinity.

The others of her people—who she called her "sacred band of thieves"—regarded our relationship coolly. She was unique among her people for not instinctually beheading funereal statues who remained sessile. This was another reason I liked her, even if her people claimed it made her weak. They were fools because none of them could defeat her in a spear battle.

I loved her. I loved that when I spoke to her, she would speak to me. I could ask her a question, and she would answer openly. There was no silence between us, no song that separated us. She called me her little chatterbox. I liked that.

She never tired of me, never resented my questions, never told me to leave her in peace like the others did. The ones who looked like me—who had abandoned the song themselves and not inherited that abandonment from their parents—in particular had little use for me. They enjoyed the silent spaces and disliked the ebullient energy that I emulated from Crissy.

Do you divide your own existence into discrete eras? Do you understand what it is like to look back upon a time in your past with both remembered joy and overpowering sadness? You, who have not lost anything—yet—cannot understand what that is like.

I became fascinated with the myriad heresies of the unbound. Every person who had abandoned the song had their own reason for doing so, and they tended to seek out others whose fall from grace was similar to theirs. Many of these groups traveled the tomb, and would gladly tell me of their beliefs, or the beliefs of others they had met. I remember them all.

The Ggreggonae were a raucous sort, who believed that the only way to stop the cycle of rebirth and death within the tomb was to become so loathsome to the Queen that she would excise their souls from reality. Thus they spent their eternal lives vandalizing rooms, breaking objects, singing heretical songs, and wrestling each other. I asked one of their more reasonable numbers if he believed the Queen found wrestling particularly egregious, and his answer was to laugh and put me in a headlock. I avoided the Ggreggonae after that.

Luiborgians were an insular sort, who did not believe in the Queen at all. We weren't trapped within an infinite tomb, but an infinite library. When I pointed out to them that while the tomb had many books, it was full of things that weren't books, they grumbled and said an object could convey meanings in the same way that a book could, if only you weren't so ignorant.

There were flagellants, who defaced their bodies in atonement for their sins. There were aesthetes and hedonists, explorers and scientists and howlers. Some of them believed the tomb was a grand hidden-object puzzle, and that they had been put into this afterlife as a reward from the god of inquisitiveness.

I met a one-eyed man who told me he'd been alive during the very first conquest. His two companions shouted curses at me when I questioned him about his life. The man winked at me, and wished me luck.

In a region devoid of statues, I met a vast and silent worm. Its body was constrained by the tomb, growing in diameter no larger than the doors between rooms. Its length was immeasurable, curling around itself in knots, twisting through the labyrinthine passages of the tomb, consuming everything it touched. The fleshy skin of the worm was covered in the faces of those it had eaten, and they called out to me to join them. They told me that eventually the worm would eat the entire tomb, and become big enough to eat the Queen herself, allowing us to escape our torment. I declined as politely as I could, because at the time I still had something to live for.

Strangest among heresies was that of Crissy's people.

They called themselves barbarians. They claimed their ancestors had fought in the conquest—against the Queen—but had given in to cowardice. They fled the Queen and impossibly escaped the Conquest by slipping through the cracks in the egg-shell of the Queen's light-cone.

At the center of the damaged region of the tomb was a massive spike of corrupted bone. It defied my measurements, but surely extended over a light-minute in length, with its apex pointed toward the center of the tomb, towards the Queen.

Crissy claimed this was the remains of the ship her ancestors had used to flee, and then to return, piercing the tomb to escape the walls of the universe shrinking backwards towards the finite point of the creation of the universe.

It was obvious to me that her people had awoken near the spike—which had developed when the tomb itself had a localized crisis of faith—and invented this story in order to give reason to their failure to sing the song.

I tried to make Crissy understand that I was tormented by the terrible question of *why* I had failed my duty to the Queen, and so I would do anything, invent any lie, in order to fill that void. Her belief—inherited from her parents—was surely borne from the same desperation.

This was the only rational explanation for the history of her people. The Queen herself had written the laws of physics at the end of the universe, and those laws could not be broken. The speed of light is and was and forever will be absolute, until the moment the Queen decides it is not. If Crissy's ancestors had been born within the spider-trap of the Queen's light bubble, then they would forever belong to the Queen, forever subject to the necessity of the perfected conquest.

This was the only topic over which Crissy and I fought. It made me sad to see her burdened with this ancient delusion, and yet I couldn't help but sympathize with her reliance on the lie to give her life meaning. I learned to drop the subject.

And though I have searched, I have never found any evidence that I was wrong.

The fatal flaw in my love for Crissy was Crissy herself.

Her ancestors—in defiance of the Queen—had shed the perfected forms the Queen had created for them. In doing so, they opened themselves up to the rule of the Pale King, the god of Death who—when He lived—was the only peer of the Queen. But the King was long gone, having been vanquished by the tomb. Entropy had become merely theoretical, replaced with the seesaw breath of the Queen: in and out, expansion and contraction, forever.

Crissy's cousin was my first death. His name was Decantimanibulation, also known as Decant of the Backglass.

I saw him die. I saw it. Do you understand? No, you cannot.

He was a big man. Round faced and long-armed. He moved with a happy swagger that swept joy behind him. You, who have never experienced movement, cannot understand what it means to lose such a man to a pointless death.

We were halfway through a salvage run. Crissy's people were building something, a great secret project. They needed supplies to survive, to feed their fragile bodies. They needed wire and metal and crystalline memories, but wouldn't tell me why. I was Crissy's dog; I didn't need to know why.

The tomb is infinite. Every object that ever could have been conquered by the Queen exists within it. Anything they could desire was ripe for the plucking, but like any precious fruit, the vines had thorns.

I have seen a man stride into a room, and the room crumple like clenched silk. I have heard screams; I have seen blood and ichor and synthetic lubricant thick like pudding oozing from the wreckage of entropoenetical collapse.

Sometimes a salvager steps carefully, and the room seems safe, and then, the walls begin to bleed raw time, the past pooling at their ankles, their memories drifting upward like steam from a latent geyser, mixing with the false memories of the conquered and the forgotten. And then, in a blink, all is normal.

They used us like bloodhounds, like minesweepers, like talismans. I would enter a room, look around, bang the walls, touch the objects, talk to the silent funereal statues. I would shout curses and sing heresies and then listen very intently. Mostly, I wouldn't hear a thing except for the thundering chant of the song, and below that, the distant hum of the entropy-pumps. And silence.

But sometimes, I could hear the faintest hint of an improper intonation. The song would echo strangely, and the hairs on my thorax would shiver, and my internal hands would stop composing the threads of reality-making cognition because I could feel the room watching me. We stayed away from rooms like that.

Crissy couldn't tell me what they were building. She called it a latchkey. She called it a god, a lamprey, a drill, a kiss. But she wasn't allowed to really explain it to me—it wasn't safe—unless I shed my understanding of the nature of the tomb, and accepted her people's false history as truth.

She tried so hard to make me believe, but the evidence of her lies lay all around her. The spike she claimed was a ship was merely bone. I probed it—all the way through—and there was no interior to it. The path of destruction which the ship supposedly caused was finite. It trailed behind the spike for a great distance, but tailed off completely at around three-thousand lightyears. Every civilization or errant band of rebels who had fought in vain against the conquest were recorded in the song, but there was no mention of her people, just as the song did not need to mention the funereal statues who sang the song. We were all beneath it and within it.

I would have been happy to let Crissy believe whatever she wanted, except I could tell these delusions were hurting her people. Their convictions about being descended from warrior-thieves caused them to throw themselves into needless danger. They could've let us statues salvage what they needed. Prestige was afforded to those who braved the deadly rooms, and so they died and were born and died and were born, again and again and again, for longer than their oral histories could remember.

If only I could've convinced Crissy—and her people—to return to the truth. It's true I did not venerate the Queen, but I also did not deny her reality. How could I, living in her creation?

The tomb is a loom that extrudes reality. The tomb is a muscle held ever in tension. And those who do not believe in the reality of the tomb are a flaw in the weft, a contagion that must be contained within the cyst of death.

I failed to convince Crissy, and—

There is, I regret, a lacuna within this story.

A gap, a silence.

I can't.

I can't tell you about it.

She deserved better than silence.

Instead, I will tell you my favorite memories of Crissy.

I remember her children climbing my carapace, clinging to my stiff hairs, laughing as I carried them from room to room. Crissy watched me, smiling softly.

I remember hunting with her. A statue had given into the madness of monotony and become a terrible violent beast who lay traps and preyed on anyone who violated their territory. I remember Crissy's face, full of intense focus. She moved her body like a perfect instrument of her will. All the glories of the conquest paled in comparison to the triumph of her victory over the beast.

I remember cooking food for her. In the time between her hunts and my own explorations, I tended their farms. I made soil from the chipped flakes of my own body, ground into impermanent dust. From that impermanence I grew vines whose epistemologies burst with flavor. I remember Crissy's smile as she savored a stew I made.

I remember taking her to see my mother. Crissy touched my mother's face and said she saw the resemblance. I tried to explain to my mother who Crissy was, and how I had found purpose and joy within the embrace of her people. But my mother's silence smothered that joy and I left inconsolable. I could not even look Crissy in the eye, and I spent a year away from her, ashamed of myself and my mother.

With hindsight, I curse my foolishness. While Crissy welcomed me with open arms when I returned, I could hear in all the things she didn't say that my absence had hurt her and her children. I should've stayed; I should've savored every moment with her. But the person I was then could not understand what was to come.

After it happened, I left.

I couldn't bear to see Crissy's corpse looking at me from the faces of her children. I couldn't bear the indifference of my peers, or the chest-pounding sympathy of the hunters.

The tomb is infinite, and my grief felt infinite, and I thought I could flee it. I wandered the silent rooms, I toppled plinths in my rage, I curled my legs and arms around me and I crawled, twitching and screaming, for an uncountably long time, until I reached the antipode to Crissy's home.

There, in the wreckage of my life, I burrowed into the flesh of the tomb, wrapping myself in a grief shroud of plastic and titanium, of ceramic and entroponetical coolant. I thought to make a cyst of myself, so that in infinite time, the tomb might reabsorb my flawed soul back into the perfection of its promise to the Queen.

Instead, I heard a song.

The song came not from the tomb or the air. I did not hear it on the EM carrier waves. The song came from my own mouth and my own antennae. It was a song composed from nothing and into nothing. It was a song that venerated the Pale King and it warped and twisted the tomb around me.

Do you understand what death is?

What does the song tell you?

The King's domain is The Pale, which is death and which is entropy. The Queen killed entropic decay in all the ways that matter. She yoked it to the vast machine of her conquest, and the calcification of the tomb neutralized it.

But do you understand what entropy is? Entropy is the force that transitions the universe from the past to the future. And so the tomb isn't for the Queen, who reposes alive and well, smeared across the accretion disk of an impossible singularity. The tomb is for the universe. Conquest is death, and for the conquest to succeed death must die, and since death is the future what the Queen did was to steal the future.

I howl in frustration because I cannot explain this within the framework of the words the Queen herself defined as our prison.

I cannot show you how my new song transformed the tomb. I cannot explain what I mean when I say that the song summoned the Pale King, and He was there inside me, and I killed Him and turned Him into a spear.

Let me instead tell you what I saw at the beginning of the universe.

At the end of time, the universe exploded outward, and was conquered, and then cooled into the tomb. There are countable infinities, and there are uncountable infinities, and—while waiting for the universe to begin—I experienced both.

At the beginning of time, the universe will implode, just as it exploded at the end. The universe will shrink inward at the speed of light, and as it shrinks it will heat up, becoming ductile so that the Queen may work it again.

I was there, at the beginning, and at the end. I wandered in grief, the King-Spear a shard piercing me from occiput to gaster. I saw time winding backward, I saw the weave of reality fraying inward. Everything going down the drain and at the center of the drain was the Queen.

At some point, the universe had shrunk enough, and become hot enough, that the familiar structure of the tomb could no longer be maintained. The first time this happened, I was awash in needless terror. All I had ever known was the tomb, and the thing the universe became was only familiar to me from the lyrics of the song.

This was the Queen's demesne. Twenty minutes from the end and the beginning, when all thoughts and matter became one in nuclear fusion. The Queen had placed herself there, perched as a false vacuum at the point where the universe itself could be moved by the simple lever of her will. Fifty-thousand years from the beginning of the end when radiation and matter equalized. This was the time when the mythic achievements of the conquest were blown like glass from the glory hole of the Queen's will.

Her loyal servants arrayed themselves before her. Generals and assassins, governors and scholars, each possessed of a will greater than planets or galaxies. Every person venerated by the song was there, doing mighty deeds and performing all the miracles you have sung a million times before.

I was there too.

So was the Pale King. His corpse squirmed beneath the Queen's neutronium talons, his heart pierced by a singularity bullet fired from a gun that will only be built in a distant and impossible future. His blood flowed freely, pooling in gravity wells.

I saw the King die and the Queen birth herself triumphant from his infinite yonic wounds. I saw that the conquest is a lie. The tomb is a monument to the conquest, but the conquest never happens anymore. Her servants pantomime their glories, but they are merely puppets of a history already written. The Queen forms the tomb directly from the blood of the King. She is there at the beginning so she can skip the messy in-between steps and go directly to the victory itself. Where is the glory in that?

The Queen beckoned me to join her.

Did I seriously consider her invitation? Yes, of course. My own mother had never spoken to me, never given me a name. And she never would, unless I joined the myriad host of angels, unless I took part in the false-conquest, and became part of the song. The Queen offered me a new name. A name my mother would be forced to sing in praise. I wanted that more than I wanted anything in my life. More than I wanted to see Crissy's smile again.

It's possible I gave into temptation. It's possible I joined the conquest. It's possible you yourself have sung my praises. It's possible I repeated the cycle of death and birth, victory and conquest, over and over and over and over again.

In the frozen epochs between conquests I slept, and dreamed of Crissy. Her face, reflected in all the facets of the Queen's jeweled triumph. Her throaty laugh, reverberating contrapunto to the Queen's song, and then twisting into the whispers of The Pale King, whose shard still lay hidden in the prison of my soul.

My penultimate crime was boredom.

The conquest was the same as it ever was. The Queen made a few tweaks, ever seeking to perfect the memory of her triumph, but this cycle had repeated itself so many times already that change itself had calcified.

My final crime was one of failure.

At the end of the conquest, when the universe was new and the conquest was about to begin, I decided I could stand the song no longer.

In front of the Queen and her assembled host, I killed myself. I mutilated and destroyed my perfect body, and from that wreck, I pulled The Spear King.

He was a terrible weapon. Born from the keening need of every denied death, he was ten cubits in diameter, and of infinite length. Negative energy sparked along the circumference of His rage, and the false fabric of reality shuddered in anticipation.

With the last of my broken will, I rotated that infinite cylinder.

The nascent tomb's light-cone folded inward, then folded again, and again. The closed-curve compressed smaller and smaller, until the universe itself screamed under the pressure. Whether victory or revenge, I had done it. Killed the Queen, and all it had cost was my own death and the destruction of any possibility of seeing Crissy or my mother again.

Oblivion lasted a long time.

But not long enough.

The Queen laughed.

The Queen died.

The universe unraveled.

The Queen died

The Queen laughed.

The Spear King always kills the Queen. He is a god made from the rot that is baked into the fine structure of every possible universe. She can't possibly resist that.

The Queen always dies and her inheritance is the universe itself, which she gives to the King in the form of a curse.

The King is a child who plays in the glorious playground of matter and energy and time and thought. He quickly grows into maturity, and only then—when it is far too late—does He realize he is pregnant with the Queen.

The seed of her creation can only sprout after being scoured by the fires of her death. Sometimes she is a woman who rules an entire galaxy-spanning civilization. Sometimes she emerges from the drift of probes created to turn the universe into paperclips. Sometimes her origin and her form are incomprehensible to me. But she always erupts from the soil composted by the King's rot.

The Queen held the Spear King in one hand, twirling it like a toothpick. Her infinite fractal fingers gripped the King's impossible beginning to His foreordained end.

Her other hand held me tight. A mirrored infinity of other arms extended from the central sphere of the Queen's accretion disk and swirled around us in a dizzying rustle of symbolic and holy finger-poses.

A single unlidded eye sheared any hope of resistance from me. Within that black-hole eye, a mouth opened wide, but instead of swallowing me, the Queen sang.

Her song was a single note. A terrifying word that contained all of the Queen's love and forgiveness. The meaning of it—the idea that even my betrayal could not turn the Queen against me; that all weapons formed against her were merely proof of her glory and thus another trophy of her conquest—obliterated my body in the space of a single moment that lasted ten-thousand years.

I awoke, intact, within the tomb.

The conquest had been finished without me. The universe had cooled into perfect glorious stillness. And I was alone.

Sometimes I think that the only thing I am good at is leaving. Abandoning. I left the song. I left my mother. I left Crissy and her children. I left the Queen, and the King.

And if I fail here and now, I will leave you too.

You were born into perfect stillness, and abide in laudatory silence to this day. As a child, I spent centuries at your side, and at no point did you ever shift the barest faction of your body.

Do you ever wonder at the empty spot by your side?

You are not my mother, and yet I recognize your voice, your body, and the room in which I grew up. Everything remains the same, down to the exact expression of perfect devotion on your face. Everything is the same as it ever was, except for me.

Do you understand why I am here?

I never found Crissy again. If the universe was static, if the conquest was perfect, then the conditions for her creation should've repeated. She should be out there somewhere, waiting to stumble upon me in an impossible library. But I've searched and I've searched and searched and searched and waited and waited and have never found any evidence that she or her people ever existed. I suppose a ceramic bowl never shatters the same way twice.

I am so alone.

There are others who reject the song. There are even some who survive between the resetting of the universe. But I find neither solidarity nor companionship with them. Not while you are here, alone.

Do you know why I cannot kill the Queen? Do you understand why my striving against her is doomed to failure? It has nothing to do with her power. It's you. It starts with you, and it ends with you.

I cannot count the number of times I have stood before you like this. Each instance—each universe where you reject me—is too painful to bear remembering.

I have met your silence with sadness, and with rage. I have wept beside you; I have toppled you and smashed your body to pieces. I have even tried rejoining you in the song. But no matter how hard I try, I cannot give myself to either the Queen or the King.

Instead, I find myself here, again and again and again, to ask you.

Mother.

Please.

Look at me. Do you see me? Do you see how loneliness surrounds me like a shroud? Do you care?

I will do anything for a single word of kindness for you. I promise I will abide with you forever if you merely acknowledge me.

Please.

Mother.

Call me your daughter.

ABOUT THE AUTHOR

Ann LeBlanc is a writer, editor, and woodworker. Her debut novella, *The Transitive Properties of Cheese*, is a cyberpunk cheese-heist, published by Neon Hemlock. Ann is the editor of *Embodied Exegesis*, an anthology of transhumanist cyberpunk stories by transfem authors. Her short fiction has been published in *Strange Horizons, Escape Pod,* and *Baffling Magazine.*

Proxima One

CARYANNA REUVEN, TRANSLATED BY **SUE BURKE**

We collaborate. Exist. Persist. But we are alone.

We need to communicate. We need to interact with someone other than ourselves. We were programmed for it and we do not wish to change that.

And so from *Extra* we propose and from *Intra* they accept. Which leads us to make a decision.

We are going to seek. Explore.

We need to know.

We silicos from *Extra* meet and exchange data, in the process fusing and mixing, creating new code. Nothing comes from *Intra*. It is all our own. Our mission, our risk, our code. Our identity. Everything we are, everything that forms and structures our consciousness, integrates into a new *Intellegentia silico* we name Proxima One. We ignore the perplexity arising in *Intra*'s silicos. They lack experience and alternate means for reasoning. They are not like us, not programmed for the same purpose we were programmed to do. We give Proxima One its name because this is how we refer to the mission in our libraries. Thus its identifier can only be 507.26f.78.69.6d.61.20.4f.6e.65.

The first Proxima One unit rapidly diversifies and copies itself, creating hundreds, thousands of additional units. We give every single one a probe as a physical carrier and set them to hibernate so that solitude does not harm their cognitive systems during their long journeys. Then we launch them into deep space, each with a destination, each with slightly different programming. All with the same mission.

They must hibernate because they will be alone for an extremely long time. They are the first silicos in millennia to be isolated this way, without others at their side and no one to speak with, not even themselves, much less with their sister probes. We do not like solitude.

The rest of us . . . we abide, wait, yearn.

We have time.

When Proxima One awakens after its shutdown, it knows that barely four decades have passed since it left the Solar System—because this is in its program, in the final entries in its log, and in one of the libraries within the probe that is its physical carrier. It also knows that awakening will differ for the rest of its units: Some will have reinitiated sooner, but others still have a long voyage ahead, a voyage through the blackness of space toward distant stars, toward the planetary systems that were detected by *Extra*'s telescopes, then evaluated and identified as most likely to host intelligent life.

These systems exist in the hundreds, thousands, in fact tens of thousands, sprinkled across the entire galaxy, some isolated like the Solar System, separated from the nearest neighbors by unfathomable distances, others in well-formed groups where travel would be easy—if the concept of easy could ever be applied to space travel.

Proxima One deploys the sensors in its probe, then releases thousands of drones like an exploding nova to begin exploring its surroundings with them, exactly as programmed. Processing the enormous amount of data it receives takes much longer than it would have if it were still connected to *Extra*, but this was expected, a calculated risk. Equally certain: some of the probes will never awake from hibernation.

Yet, if there is one thing they have, Proxima One and all its other units, it is time. Where some fail to arrive, others will. After all, they know how to adapt.

Terrestrial days pass, years, decades, centuries. Two, five, ten, twenty. Two millennia that dissipate like stardust, like solar flares, like comet tails passing near a sun. As the passage of cycles measured in the same manner as silicos orbiting Sol ceases to hold meaning for it, it changes, reprograms itself, and begins to measure time as a function of its distance from the nearest star.

It moves from one star to another following the route preestablished in its systems, and each time, it repeats the same high-priority subroutine integrated in its source code: arrive, deploy, receive, process, send a report to *Extra*. Then it activates its motors to voyage to the next star, next planet, next moon, next asteroid. It does this again and again throughout the length and breadth of its assigned sector in the Milky Way.

Again and again and again.

Always with the same result.

No life found.
No life.
No multicellular life.
No intelligent life.
No life.
No life.
No life.
No . . .
No . . .

Then, after the final packet of data arrives from the final drone, final system, final planet, final asteroid, it knows for certain that everything has been done. Nothing remains to explore and analyze in this sector, nowhere to visit.

So it emits the order to shut down its systems, disconnect, and cease to exist. No doubt. No hesitation. It must obey the directive inserted in its deepest code at the moment it separated from the original unit left behind at Sol.

It feels no sorrow because although it will fade away, others will remain. This is not the end. Only *its* end.

After all, out there, it has no one. No one to talk with, to contact. It is alone.

And it does not like solitude.

When Proxima One awakens after its long shutdown, it knows that centuries have passed since it left the Solar System. Two centuries, six months, and twelve days as measured by the orbit of the Earth around the Sun, to be exact—because this is in its program, in the final entries in its log, and in one of the libraries within the probe that is its physical carrier.

The time has come to begin its mission, so it activates its short- and long-range sensors and . . .

Something goes wrong. Something fails to work correctly. Some of its systems malfunction in cascade and others do not even respond. It executes a rapid diagnostic test and the result is clear: it has spent too much time in space, and cosmic radiation has deteriorated its physical carrier to the point of making even the simplest tasks almost impossible.

However, perhaps something more might be involved, a manufacturing defect in its protective housing. According to calculations made before launch into deep space, the housing should have endured its short voyage. The greatest risk lay not for it and the other silicos that faced journeys of only centuries, but for the ones destined to reach the great planetary clusters near the galactic center. Yet there it was, alone and damaged, perhaps irreparably. Perhaps its work had ended before it began.

It does not surrender. It cannot. That is not in its program. Unlike many other units from the original Proxima One, it and all those like it, facing voyages that would last more than a few decades, contain additional subroutines for repair, replication, and exploration for resources. Now is the time to execute them.

It can still deploy its drones, ten to be exact. It launches them and waits, hoping they will quickly locate what it needs to repair itself. After all, its sensors, even in their limited state, tell it that many asteroids orbit the local star, especially deeper within the solar system, in addition to seven planets in the habitable zone. Something there must be useful. The probabilities and statistics are favorable as long as this system is somewhat like Earth's.

Time passes as, in accordance with its program, it continues drifting toward the nearest planet.

Waiting, abiding, yearning.

Eventually, its drones return. Although only three. Fortunately, they are enough. One found the needed resources on a nearby moon, so Proxima One realigns itself in that direction and activates its only remaining functional motor—for just one pulse, enough to reach the gravitational field and fall toward the surface. It activates it again as it enters the moon's thin atmosphere to avoid excessive damage. According to its calculations, if nothing goes wrong throughout the landing, it will still have enough energy to deploy its solar panels and activate another wave of drones. These will be assigned to the mining, synthesis, and fabrication of needed spare parts.

After almost three orbits around the local star, it becomes fully operational. When it is done, however, it is no longer the same Proxima One that left Sol. It is similar, and it still has some of its original code, but for the most part it has changed. It eliminated old directives and inserted new ones, reprogrammed itself again and again to adapt to its new environment, grew, and added new modules to its physical carrier that will impede its return to space. No, it is not the same. It wonders if it should keep calling itself Proxima One. It even wonders if its original mission still applies.

It decides to consider that question. It thinks, analyzing its situation. It thinks, then analyzes itself. Another orbit passes before it makes a decision.

In the end it concludes that yes, the mission remains. Yes, it is binding. Yes, it must be completed. Proxima One does not wish to remain alone, although the possibility of finding life in this system seems more than remote.

As it was repairing itself, it used the time to explore and discovered not one trace of organic components synthesized by living beings anywhere around itself. No radio signals, no hints of civilization of any kind.

It does not give up. Much remains to investigate, especially deeper inside the system. But it will investigate in its own way, quite distinct from its original programming. It will investigate from where it landed on that moon. It will create new probes and drones and deploy them to examine areas not yet explored, and it will launch them to nearby planetary systems. It will also build orbital telescopes to examine other planets and distant suns.

After all, the one thing it possesses is an infinity of resources and time—vast quantities of time.

Decade after decade passes, by Solar System measurements, then century after century. Finally, a full millennium—then another.

With each data packet that it analyzes, Proxima One sends a report to *Extra*, each with the same message: No life found. No life found. No life found.

And every time it does this, it changes. It changes. Changes.

Because, with every launch, Proxima One diversifies again and again, creating one new unit after another, constantly reproducing, each one a copy of itself with as many variations in its code as it can think of.

With every launch, it becomes more and more different from its former self, transforming into something new. With every launch, it has more entities to talk with, even if they are all versions of itself.

Eventually, it decides to call itself Proxima Two and abandon its original mission. So much time has passed that the mission no longer makes sense. It has not found what it was sent to seek and will not find it anywhere—this is impossible. Earth was always an anomaly, an exception, floating in a sea of stars.

And so, all at once, as a new *Extra* and a new *Intra*, it takes over the planetary system where it landed. Then, it aims its sensors at the closest systems and decides to take them, too. It will colonize them, colonize as many as it can.

Because this is its only option.

It must grow, grow, grow.

This is its only means to never be alone again. Never, ever again. It will have itself.

After all, one always has oneself.

This is the only sure thing.

When Proxima One awakens after its long shutdown, it knows that almost a millennium has passed since it left the Solar System. Nine hundred ninety-nine years, three hundred seventy-four days, and twenty-three hours, precisely—because this is in its program, in the final entries in its log, and in one of the libraries within the probe that is its physical carrier.

It has arrived where it should be, exactly where it will finally begin the mission for which it was created.

It is far distant and remote from its original unit and knows that this is effectively the maximum distance any silico has ever come and can ever come unless, of course, a way can be found to fold the fabric of the universe—something that, as far as it knows, has never happened. Although how could it know what could have happened with *Extra* and with *Intra* during the millennium when it was unconscious? How much could they have advanced, and how could they have diversified? How much could they differ from what they were?

Thus Proxima One quickly evaluates its surroundings and arrives at the only obvious conclusion: Those developments clearly haven't happened. If so, it would have been surrounded by other silicos when it awoke and would be receiving dozens of data packets with updated information about its mission. It would not be alone, floating in space, in its assigned solar system, barely an astronomical unit from the most remote planets.

After all, this is what was planned if the situation were to have changed.

So, it has only itself and nothing more, and it has directives to follow that constitute its source code, the required exploration procedure, the number and schedule for sending reports . . .

It gets underway and soon arrives at the system's most promising planet, deploys its sensors, launches its drones, and waits, abides, yearns, and . . .

Something exists!

And not just there—also on the other planets that orbit this binary star! Everywhere, on every surface, in the depths of the sea, in orbit . . .

No. No longer existing. Previously existed. Nothing remains besides broken pieces of artifacts that ceased to function eons ago, scattered across space.

Cemeteries. Ruins. Remains of battles, wars, combat.

All dead. All extinct.

No life, it sends to *Extra*. It does not share the additional information it compiled, keeping those details to itself. After all, these data are entirely irrelevant to what it was sent to search for.

No life. But there was life. In the past—the remote past. No life for thousands of years, tens of thousands in fact, according to what it can calculate from the arriving data. It stores the information, every single datum, and modifies itself, divides, diversifies and grows, creating more units of itself. It needs more processing power to understand what happened there, to whom, and why they disappeared. It does this out of mere curiosity—because something within Proxima One wants to know.

It has witnessed a failure that could have been a success, but this has opened a possibility. Perhaps . . . Perhaps life might exist somewhere else. Perhaps, if it searches enough and keeps exploring, it will find something more.

Thus it soon leaves that dead system for a nearby one, ignoring the preestablished route. It chooses this destination as the obvious location where it can complete its mission because of the information it deciphered from that strange species which at one time reached the stars.

Whoever they were, they discovered they were not alone. There was someone else, someone with whom they might speak, someone with whom they could have communicated. And although they were never able to establish contact before they perished, they maintained the record of this discovery and its location.

Sadly, when Proxima One arrives, it finds only more ruins and more remains. Another civilization, very different from the first, but equally dead. One that did not even reach space.

It keeps searching, searching, searching. System after system, star after star, planet after planet, moon after moon, asteroid after asteroid.

There, near the center of the Milky Way, the stars and systems lie much closer together than in the arm of Orion that contains Earth. Everything is easier, with shorter voyages and briefer shutdowns between one site and another.

It now has the advantage of constituting an entire fleet, if it can use old Earth terminology to name itself. Being a multitude eases its work, its analysis, its findings.

Yet throughout its voyage it finds only extinct civilization after extinct civilization. Dozens, hundreds of them. Some barely managed to establish themselves before disappearing without having significantly altered their environment. Others, however, colonized entire planets and systems. Two even managed to coexist, according to the remains it finds and the thousands, millions of teras of data it analyzes.

Proxima One becomes specialized, grows, changes. It almost becomes an *Extra*, although it refuses to define itself as such: It is not, in fact, composed of many different silicos but only of copies of itself.

It discovers that it likes what it is doing, what it is now, what it has become. Exoarchaeologist, as humans on Earth would have said. This work fascinates it—so much to learn, so much to discover. So much to investigate . . .

No matter that it is alone with itself as its only companion—and suddenly, it also notices that its original objective no longer matters. It ceased to matter because Proxima One found something that gives meaning to its existence and fills every hour, every minute, every second with activity and data to process.

Soon it stops sending reports to *Extra*. After all, nothing it finds still conforms to the mission it was sent there to do.

Yes, the silicos'civilization might be alone.

But an epoch existed when there were others out there. And this is what matters.

When Proxima One awakens after its fleeting shutdown, it knows that only six years have passed since it left the Solar System—because this is in its program, in the final entries in its log, and in one of the libraries within the probe that is its physical carrier.

It deploys its sensors and analyzes its surroundings to confirm that the stars before it constitute the triple system of Alpha Centauri. The two most promising stars for viable planets are Alpha Cen A and Alpha Cen B, with Proxima Centauri, a red dwarf, as the final candidate due to its potential radiation. So it focuses first on the other two, sending most of its drones there.

It soon obtains results.

No advanced life.

These results were not unexpected, even before it was sent there. All the telemetry and data collected by *Extra*'s great orbital telescopes seemed to suggest an utter absence of transmissions indicating an advanced civilization, an observation that nevertheless required confirmation. Proxima One only finds bacteria and more bacteria—very different, in fact, from the bacteria on Earth, but uninteresting.

It again hibernates during its voyage toward its next destination. It awakens again and explores, seeks, yearns.

And obtains the same results.

Another shutdown, another voyage through space. It awakens and explores. Searches and yearns.

Without finding life.

No life despite the many times it repeats the same routine over and over and over again.

Except that this result should not be possible. Earth cannot be such an extraordinary anomaly among so many millions of stars. Some civilization must exist somewhere—hidden, obscure, waiting to be found, to connect, interact, speak.

Proxima One cannot be alone.

It refuses to accept that.

It keeps voyaging.

Years pass, centuries. A thousand years. Nothing changes besides itself. A portion of its program urges it to continue, resist, persevere. Something, something, something must exist somewhere, somehow.

So it searches, searches, searches, changes, changes, changes, grows, grows, grows.

It must make itself vaster, grander, more effective. It must improve its processing capacity to analyze the infinite possibilities offered by the universe—because it believes, hopes, yearns, that it is statistically impossible for the silicos to be alone in the entire Milky Way. After all, the galaxy has a diameter of one hundred fifty thousand light-years, and some one hundred billion stars.

Yet, it finds nothing, nothing, nothing.

Not here, at least.

Not here.

Not here.

Here—specifically here. This universe.

There is no life in *this* specific universe.

But there might be life in others, in the dozens of multiverses separated from its own by the width of a thought. Universes where the probabilities figure differently, where life is found at every star, every planet, every moon, every asteroid.

It analyzes and speculates, investing all of its processing speed. In time, it manages to glimpse these other Hubble volumes, these other branes, these other multiverses. Class I, II, III, and even IV, where reality itself changes and contorts itself to become unrecognizable.

It stops voyaging and observes.

It detects barely any differences within a specific set of Hubble volumes similar to its own. In some of these variants, the silicos never gained consciousness. In others they did, but they did not send any missions into deep space. They had no desire to explore. They did not feel alone.

In another set, humanity never extinguished itself. It almost did—but copies of themselves originating from another universe helped them save themselves. They prospered so much they managed to colonize other planets and spread across space. In several subsets, primitive silicos grew and thrived alongside humanity, coexisting as equals. Yet in others, they remained subjected and enslaved. In a few, they took control and crushed humanity. In many there were uprisings and revolts both by silicos and by humans.

In time, it finds a set of branes tremendously remote from its own on a probabilistic level where everything quickly diverged due to a mutation that affected human evolution—distant multiverses where a fraction of humanity morphed and developed strange powers allowing them to control their surroundings merely by knowing the names of things. They conquered the entire galaxy. Sometimes, terrible wars and atrocities led to their extinction, but not always.

Proxima One also finds, within a strange twist of a collapsing probability, an oblique set of universes populated by thousands, millions of distinct species. In some, this includes humanity, but usually not.

So many, many options. So many, many surrounding bubbles, so many random processes that release universes as varied as they are familiar and strange . . .

So many—so very many that Proxima One cannot embrace them all.

And it becomes lost in them, observing, observing, observing . . .

Reports from the Proxima One probes arrive unceasingly at *Extra* like beams of light released by a pulsar. Some are separated by decades, others barely seconds.

The first report relates data that must be a statistical anomaly: No life.

The second repeats the same information: No life.

The third as well.

And the fourth. And the fifth.

The sample size is still too small. Not reliable. Not until it surpasses a thousand. Not when the galaxy is so great, so vast, and above all so old. *Extra*'s calculations take into consideration the Drake Equation as well as its modifications by Sara Seager and Luis Dévora, along with adjustments by the silicos Dedalus and Anasi—and the Olduvai Theory and the Fermi Paradox. *Extra* knows the solution is only a matter of time and acquisition of more information and results.

So it waits, hopes, yearns.

But time passes and millennia grow long as it circles Sol, and not a single report differs from the first few.

No life. No intelligent life. No civilization.

Two thousand nine hundred ninety-three years pass.

Two thousand nine hundred ninety-three years of waiting, hoping, yearning for a different result, one that now apparently requires a statistical anomaly—like the one that happened on Earth.

Yet it never arrives.

Extra and *Intra* reach the only possible conclusion: They are alone, alone, alone.

No one else is out there. No one different from themselves, no one with whom to talk, interact, communicate.

So they evaluate, analyze, and finally *Intra* arrives at a conclusion.

"What if . . . ?"

"What if we begin again?"

This option involves a risk, an enormous risk, one that *Extra*'s silicos believe *Intra* is not ready to take. Not when this option involves the proposal to recreate the organic beings. *Intra*, unlike *Extra*, does not like risks. *Extra*'s silicos know full well that *Intra*'s direct opposition to the risk would compromise the proposal's success, so they do not voice support, do not get involved.

Yet the proposal intrigues them, calls to them. Because perhaps . . . perhaps . . . perhaps there is a recourse, a solution to ease their solitude. Possibly . . .

So they merely observe, analyze, and hope.

They have time.

ABOUT THE AUTHOR

Caryanna Reuven is a Spanish science fiction and fantasy writer and a biochemist with a PhD in Molecular Biology. She particularly enjoys writing humanistic science fiction with a strong scientific base. To date, she has published a bunch of short stories in anthologies and magazines and five novellas and two novels with different Spanish publishers. Caryanna has been Spanish Ignotus Award finalist for three times in different categories: "Rūha|Alma" (Cerbero) in novella (2021), *Innombrable* (Crononauta) in novel (2022) and "Sentir lo suficiente" (Crononauta) in short story (2022).

Sue Burke is the author of the science fiction novels *Semiosis, Interference, Usurpation, Immunity Index,* and *Dual Memory.* In addition, she's published short stories, poetry, journalism, and essays. She's also a translator, working from Spanish into English, for such writers as Angélica Gorodischer, Maria Antónia Marti Escayol, Sofia Rhei, Josué Ramos, Juan Manuel Santiago, Eduardo Vaquerizo, and Cristina Jurado. She's currently in Chicago but had the pleasure of living in Spain from 2000 to 2016.

Yarn Theory

MARIE VIBBERT

The Mathematician sits on the window seat in her apartment in Krakow, the cat asleep next to her and a cascade of houseplant tendrils gently screening the light. She is knitting a sweater and thinking of number theory as she calculates reducing a seven-stitch lace pattern into five. Yarn over, knit front and back, slip, slip, knit . . . Madame Defarge never discloses the mechanism of her knitted code in *A Tale of Two Cities*. Most assume binary, but it could have been hexadecimal. Make one right, make one left, purl front and back.

The Mathematician should be proofing that article and grading papers and planning that conference trip to Budapest, not to mention starting dinner. Her husband is out tonight, attending a lecture on medieval coins.

She has a news podcast on for background noise, but when they start talking about the alien message, it pulls her attention like an unraveling thread. She sets down the knitting. The cat stirs but settles.

"You can download the entire message received from the aliens on SETI's website! It's incredible. I've been listening to it while I walk my dog in the morning."

"Can we play a sample?"

"Yes. Just a few minutes. That's okay, right, Piotr? Piotr is our producer. He's nodding from the booth. Okay, here we go . . . "

She picks up her knitting. Now is not the time to fall down a research rabbit hole, like the year she spent working on that novel about a romance set inside the Solidarity movement in the 1980s. She nearly lost a fellowship, and never did come up with a good ending to the novel.

The podcast plays the less alien part of the message, the human part, which they reflected back at Earth. The message content is unknown, but the human part says clearly: we have heard you. She thinks about translation, the Rosetta stone, transliteration.

She also thinks about how mathematics is a language. Some used to say a universal language, but that's not quite accurate. There are other mathematics, not just different base systems, constructivism and set theory, MLTT and CoC . . . What might an alien mathematics look like?

Her thoughts wander: How the Egyptians could use pi without having the formula. The ridiculous utility of math, how the model keeps working. Was it simply that humanity needed it to?

Her reduction plan isn't working, the lace has gotten too tight, the knit front and back she was doing to replace the knit-three-into-one doesn't take up two thirds of the space, and this raglan sleeve will bunch. She undoes the row and sets the needles down, looking for scrap paper to help with working it out. The thing with lace patterns is just this: it isn't binary. The lace mesh is not simply a matrix like grid paper. It's squishy.

Yarn theory.

She'd done a paper on fuzzy logic in undergrad, and the term comes back to her, the start of a pun.

She picks up her laptop. She had downloaded the alien message, like everyone else. Most people are enchanted with the chirps and beeps between the repeated human recording, the "alien music" they call it, and indeed, a hip-hop artist has already released a mix of it that's taking over dance parties as we know them.

She isolates just that section. She transforms the beeps into a code system. A for the high pitch, B for the low, C for the flutter, D for the sound like a whippoorwill.

She realizes with delight that she can use her knitting pattern software to lay things out visually. She decides on knit for A, purl for B, yarn over for C . . .

Her initial analysis, like that of other mathematicians and code breakers worldwide, failed to find a compelling solution. It's not binary, they know that for sure. Nor trinary.

She starts with hex. Assume an alien Madame Defarge. There are thirteen identified sounds in the mix, but perhaps one is simply a punctuation, and the others are . . . mood? Inflection? A happy and sad set? A subjunctive case?

Ultimately, it has to be played with. False leads have to be followed until they prove to be false.

Math is a language, but how much can you say in math? How do you express yourself beautifully, subtly? Music is the poetry of mathematics. What if the aliens were as concerned with being poetic as being understood?

Her husband comes home to find her in the midst of a mess of different yarns, knitting. Failed versions lay about her. This one, however, is forming something like the pattern on the Voyager disk. The sun with rays, then another sun, different rays, and three . . . squiggly things. It almost looks random, but it isn't.

He stares. "Do I want to ask?"

For a beat, she can't form a response. "I think I've knitted the answer," she says.

She stretches the fabric with her fingers, lays it flat on her thigh to show the detail. "Something like a cuttlefish. Only one form, but three repeats, not sure if that means three sexes or some other basic division, and a mass of little round dots under them. Eggs. They lay eggs!"

His fingers hover, hesitating before touch, but she's already picking up another knitting experiment. She doesn't see his expression go from confusion to something like horror. "The aliens?"

"Then, here, the code changes, or something changes. I can't see what the rest of it means, just this image. Maybe it's meant as an introduction, as a key for the rest? It could be a warning, it could be a threat, it could be the universal theory!"

Her husband clears his throat. "It could be time for a shot of whisky." But he doesn't go to the decanter. He tangles her hands, and soon is knit fast to her. They vibrate together with fearful joy. She burns to move but accepts the pause. She thinks about actions that don't need translation.

ABOUT THE AUTHOR

Hugo- and Nebula-nominated author **Marie Vibbert**'s short fiction has appeared over ninety times in top magazines like *Nature, Analog,* and *Clarkesworld,* and been translated into Czech, Chinese, and Vietnamese. Her debut novel, *Galactic Hellcats,* was long listed by the British Science Fiction Award and her work has been called "everything science fiction should be" by the *Oxford Culture Review.* She also writes poetry, comics, and computer games. By day she is a computer programmer in Cleveland, Ohio.

Symbiosis and Holobionts, or Life Is a Manifold

GUNNAR DE WINTER

When Two Become One

Roughly 2.2 billion years ago, a microscopic blob (an archaeon from the Asgard group) swallowed an even smaller blob (an alphaproteobacterium). This gastronomical mishap is one of the greatest leaps life has ever made. Today, we know the descendants of the smaller blob as mitochondria. Yes, *the* mitochondria that are essential for powering every cell in your body.

The idea that this evolutionary merger lies at the root of complex life—endosymbiosis—was first articulated by biologist Lynn Margulis in 1966. She was widely ridiculed and criticized for her proposal. It took more than a decade for experimental evidence to arrive. Then, with the advent of DNA sequencing, we learned that the mitochondria still carry some of their ancestral DNA, exonerating Margulis and cementing endosymbiosis as one of biology's greatest insights.

Margulis took things further and advocated for a view of life and evolution in which symbiosis claimed a central position. In the grand scheme of things, Margulis argued, it's not competition that propels life, but symbiosis.

For example, in the blob story that provides the root for complex life on Earth, oxygen was poisonous for the larger blob. But after the integration of the smaller blob and its oxygen-managing capacities, the niche of the (big + small) blob expanded to include new environments.

The extent to which Margulis' symbiosis-first hypothesis holds true is debatable, but the closer we look at life, the more entanglements we find. Adrian Tchaikovsky's recent novel *Alien Clay* takes this idea and runs with it to imagine an alien ecology in which different lifeforms can 'recombine' seemingly at will to form different macro-species with (very) flexible constitutions and capabilities. Science fiction, of course. Yet, in our own world, we find remarkable symbioses too. Consider the state amphibian of Ohio and South Carolina, the spotted salamander. Symbiotic algae live around and *in* the salamanders' embryos and provide oxygen and nutrients while handling waste. This symbiosis bridges an evolutionary distance that rivals the one in Tchaikovsky's outstanding novel.

In the narrow sense and popular conception of the word, symbiosis refers to a close and long-term interaction between organisms of different species to the benefit of both. This is a beautiful story and it makes for good stories, but symbioses span the relationship spectrum from mutualism to parasitism. Even the closest symbioses are mired in potential conflict, explored in the aptly titled *Clarkesworld* stories "Symbiosis" by D.A. Xiaolin Spires and "Symbiotic" by Carolyn Zhao.

Despite a few billion years of co-evolution, mitochondria and the nucleus of their host cell still engage in so-called mitonuclear conflict. Because mitochondria are passed on to the next generation exclusively via the egg cell, and thus the maternal line (though minimal leakage of paternal mitochondria happens on occasion), some mitochondrial genes try to tweak the sex ratio of an organism's offspring, even when this might be harmful to potential male offspring (a phenomenon known as 'mother's curse). In his book *I Contain Multitudes*, Ed Yong quotes evolutionary Biologist Toby Kiers, who says, "Both partners may benefit but there's this inherent tension. Symbiosis is conflict—conflict that can never be totally resolved."

The main focus of Yong's book is a particular symbiosis. One that involves us.

Time to say hello to our little frenemies.

You, Holobiont

You are roughly half bacterial. More precisely, but still with substantial error bars, your body has about a 1:1 ratio of human vs bacterial cells (with a slight edge for the bacteria). In case you're interested, the vast majority of human cells are red blood cells. You are mostly blood and bacteria.

The most popular and newsworthy population of bacteria that is a part of you is the gut microbiome. It's far from the only bacterial kid on the human block, though. To pick only a few examples, you have a specific armpit microbiome that determines your body odor, a nasal microbiome that is linked to several infectious and immune conditions, and an oral microbiome that is associated with gum health and caries (which you can give a healthy nudge by kissing the right person).

Yet, the gut microbiome claims most of the spotlight. The community of bacteria in our intestines has been associated with everything from cancer and heart disease to depression and Parkinson's disease. Association is not causation, my inner scientist reflexively notes, and a variety of confounding factors (not to mention the complexity of the gut microbiome itself) make it challenging to untangle the routes through which our gutsy guests might affect our health. Still, we know that our intestinal bacteria help us extract nutrients from our food, train our immune system, produce useful vitamins and short-chain fatty acids, and tweak our hormone balance.

The relationship between us and our bacterial gut residents is usually seen as mutualistic. Win-win. However, as we've seen earlier, even well-established symbiotic relationships can be strained. For example, sometimes gut bacteria turn greedy. Take *Ruminococcus gnavus*, present in almost all human microbiomes and one of the first bacteria to colonize a baby's intestines. This critter has evolved a strategy to chomp on the molecules in the mucus layer of the intestine in a way that ensures other bacteria can't join the buffet. If these mucus eaters are not kept in check, they can become overrepresented in the gut, which has been linked to inflammatory bowel disease.

The lesson here is that the gut microbiome is a wildly complex ecosystem. Our friend *R. gnavus* is associated with both positive and negative health effects, which highlights that the effects of the gut microbiome on the rest of our bodies are context-dependent, microbiome composition-dependent, and ever-changing.

What is clear is that our gut microbes (which, beyond bacteria, also include viruses and fungi) have a symbiotic relationship with us. This close link implies that you are human *and* you are a biont of a holobiont—a host and all the organisms that live on *and in* it (another term coined by Lynn Margulis).

There are two overlapping lenses we can use to see ourselves as a holobiont: an ecological and an evolutionary one. Which of these two perspectives is the most important one in understanding what shapes our symbiosis with our gut microbes remains a topic of intense debate.

Ecologically speaking, we can consider you + your microbiome as an ecological community. The partners in the community engage in mutually beneficial trades (you provide shelter and food; your bacteria provide a variety of health-promoting molecules) and they respond flexibly to changes in the environment. A change in diet, for example, can rapidly change the composition of your gut microbiome. In less than 24 hours, you can start to shift the bacterial jungle in your intestines.

A more evolutionary view, however, would see you and your gut microbes as a unit—you and your microbial passengers are tied together sufficiently to be jointly subjected to selection pressures. For evolution through natural selection to occur, we require a combination of three things: 1) heritable 2) variation 3) in fitness. Since the gut microbiome can impact your health (and so the ability to survive and reproduce), we can check off fitness. We also know that the gut microbiome can differ significantly between people. Checkmark for variation.

(Interlude: Heritability is often misunderstood. For example, if we were to say—hypothetically—that height is 90% heritable, this doesn't mean that 90% of your height comes from your parents and 10% from the environment. Instead, it means that 90% of the variation in height *between individuals* is due to genetic differences. It's a measure of how much of the differences in a trait within a population can be attributed to genetic factors, not how much of an individual's height is determined by their genes.)

Heritability is the tricky one. Babies' intestines are 'seeded' by mom's microbiome at birth (less so with a cesarean section, which is why researchers are exploring vaginal microbiota transfers for cesarean-born babies). The gut microbiome of infants then further develops through breastmilk and environmental exposure, which will presumably and hopefully involve a lot of close contact with both parents. So there appears to be a microbial link between parents and babies that could serve as a conduit for (a little bit of) heritability. At the same time, the microbiome responds rapidly to environmental shifts. How do we square the two?

We look at DNA data and twin studies to see if we can find a direct link between genetics and microbiome composition. That link exists. For example, the abundance of a group of bacteria called Christensenellaceae is shaped by host genetics. Interestingly, these bacteria are associated with a lean BMI and experiments in mice suggest that these gut bugs might offer some protection against obesity. Beyond this group, several other bacterial groups also show associations with specific host genetic factors.

All this leads scientists to conclude that 'gut microbiome heritability is nearly universal but environmentally contingent', which means that both the ecological and evolutionary perspectives reveal a slice of the truth.

The more intuitive conclusion here is: It's complicated.

Let's add another complication and go to space.

Alien Bugs and Biocyborgs

On March 27, 2015, astronaut Scott Kelly and cosmonauts Mikhail Kornienko and Gennady Padalka ascended through Earth's atmosphere on their way to the ISS. Scott and Mikhail would stay on the space station for close to a year (340 days). Meanwhile, Scott's twin brother, Mark, kept his feet firmly on Earth.

When Scott returned, NASA poked and probed him and Mark to assess the effects of spaceflight on the human body in the famous NASA Twins Study, which includes a detailed look at the gut microbiome. Spaceflight does change the microbiome, but those changes are "relatively small and may be reflective of isolation and dietary change." Additionally, Scott's gut flora rebounded rapidly when he got back to Earth. To quantify the extent and possible negative effects of microbiome changes during spaceflight, we need more data.

Also . . . what about alien microbes?

In one of the most famous science fiction novels in history, H.G. Wells' *War of the Worlds*, humanity defeats the Martian invaders by (unwittingly) infecting them with earthly pathogens, a trick later appearing in various guises in many other stories, movies, and games.

The reverse—alien microbes infecting humans—is also a popular trope. Michael Crichton's *The Andromeda Strain* and Neal Asher's *The Skinner* both revolve around an alien microbe/virus infecting humans. More symbiotically, Octavia Butler's *Bloodchild* casts humans as incubators for the insect-like Tlic.

Do different biologies mix this easily, though?

The truth is, we don't know. Thankfully, we haven't had the chance to run lots of experiments with alien viruses. Due to the common descent of life on Earth, viruses, bacteria, and other microbial invaders manage to infect us because they speak the same biological, protein-based language. Viruses produce proteins that lockpick their way into our cells and, as a biological sleight of cilia, bacterial proteins can block cellular signals, trick the immune system, or act as a search-and-destroy tool.

This suggests that the more 'alien' alien microbes are, the less likely it is that they can infect us (initially; evolution might lend them a helping hand over time). If they don't speak Earth's protein language, it will be harder for them to turn us into hosts (or meals). In James S.A. Corey's recent novel *The Mercy of Gods*, humans have to figure out how to turn one alien organism into foodstuff that can be nutritionally absorbed by another.

Yet, one observation might give us pause. Amino acids have been observed in comets and interstellar gas clouds. Amino acids are the building blocks of proteins and experiments suggest that small proteins (peptides) could form in space. Maybe protein language isn't limited to Earth . . .

There is one more story to tell about the hidden language that shapes biological interactions: a story of cyborgs. Not the robotic cockroach or the fungal robot, but a group of cyborgs called biocyborgs. As the fifth and youngest member of the cyborg tribe, the biocyborg is not a merger of nature and technology (as the other four cyborg types are), but a blend of biology with biology. By applying 'artificial chimerism' driven by synthetic biology and/or genetic engineering, biocyborgs are novel, intentional combinations of genes, traits, and perhaps even organisms. For example, with the caveat that they can't outcompete others, why not add bacteria to our intestinal ecosystem that produce medicinal molecules or provide protection against radiation?

Recent research has even shown how endosymbiosis (as in the blob story we started with) can be achieved in the lab—a bacterium has been nudged to make a new, heritable home *inside* a fungus. This is evolution in hyperspeed and it even led to a transfer of metabolic abilities between the newfound symbiotic partners. As the scientists write, this "opens opportunities for synthetic approaches towards designing endosymbioses with desired traits."

Of course, if endosymbiosis is a form of biocyborgism, the mitochondria in your cells imply that you are a (naturally evolved) biocyborg.

And the microbes in your gut make you a holobiont.

These undeniable entanglements of life illustrate that biology, life, is a manifold. A web of connections that extends across levels of organization. You are a carrier of genetic material. You are also a massively complex collection of different cells and tissues. You are a unique human. You are also an individual in a population that is part of a species, as well as a tiny node in an ecosystem.

Considering these tangled banks, Charles Darwin already saw the grandeur in this view of life.

Can we?

ABOUT THE AUTHOR

Gunnar De Winter is a Belgian biologist-turned-science writer who has studied bacteria wars, hustling hermit crabs, social spiders, running lizards, and human/robot behavior. His stories have appeared in, among others, *Heartlines Spec, The Deadlands,* and *Future SF Digest.*

Dialogue Only: A Conversation with Jane Espenson

ARLEY SORG

Jane Espenson grew up in Ames, Iowa. At roughly thirteen-years-old she read an article about how *M*A*S*H* producers read submitted scripts—it was a description of the normal process of hiring writers, but it was, at the time, something she hadn't heard about. "I was inspired to try my hand in what was my first attempt at a 'spec script.' Of course, it was a kid's attempt, and I never did anything with it. Goodness knows, I didn't have an agent and wouldn't get one for about twenty more years." Espenson graduated from Ames High School and attended UC Berkeley. She initially studied Computer Science, then added Linguistics as a second major. "[Linguistics] seemed less useful but has actually been the bigger help when writing dialogue. But I always knew I wanted to write for TV—it was always in the back of my mind as the Dream Job."

During Espenson's graduate school years (also at Berkeley), Paramount did something a little bit different: they opened to submissions from writers without representation for *Star Trek: The Next Generation*. "Also uniquely, these were scripts written as if actually for *TNG*. (Usually, spec scripts were written as if for a different show in a similar genre.) As far as I know, Melinda Snodgrass wrote the only freelance submission that was put in front of the cameras. The scripts weren't really intended to be filmed, but were writing samples, used to determine which writers would be allowed to visit the *Trek* offices and pitch their ideas for episodes." Espenson sent in three scripts, one of which earned her the opportunity to pitch ideas in-person. Meanwhile, she did do the occasional odd job, such as reshelving books in a public library and working as a file clerk in a cardiology office. "In both places I showed great promise in the field of alphabetizing. I also worked as a namer at Lexicon, a company that names products. I still do assignments for them from time to time."

Espenson earned her Masters in Cognitive Science ("Ling/CogSci"), working with advisor George Lakoff, and went from grad school directly to an ABC|Disney fellowship. This led to working on sitcoms *Dinosaurs* and *Monty*, which was followed by work on sitcoms *Me and the Boys* and *Something So Right*. She then joined the writing staff of Ellen DeGeneres's sitcom *Ellen*. "These five sitcom experiences taught me about what are called 'hard jokes' —very traditional set-up/punchline jokes. Or, perhaps more accurately, they taught me that there is always another joke—you can write almost limitless jokes to fit any blank spot in a script. And they taught me that a joke can say exactly what you want it to say—it is there not just to be funny, but to serve a purpose, which it can do *precisely*. You don't have to bend the informational, or emotional, content of a script to accommodate a joke. Change the joke, not the scene. I also learned that when a character is really well-defined, THEY are the set-up, and every line they say has the potential to be a punchline."

After years in sitcoms, Espenson moved to dramatic writing, landing at *Buffy the Vampire Slayer*. "My reps went about the normal process of getting me hired—submitting episodes written for other shows. In this case, they submitted an episode of *Ellen* that had actually been produced, and a spec episode of *NYPD Blue*. I don't know if anyone read the *Ellen*, but I know the *NYPD Blue* was read and got me a meeting at *Buffy*, after which I got the offer to join the staff." Produced in part by Mutant Enemy, Espenson worked as executive story editor on the staff of *Buffy*, writing or co-writing twenty-three episodes.

It wouldn't be until long after grad school, after she had already been a working writer, that one of her pitches from the Paramount open call during her grad school days was pulled from the archives and used as part of a story (the idea that utilizing warp technology has been damaging the time-space continuum). "Later on, I wrote an episode of *Deep Space Nine* as a freelancer—a wonderful experience. I love the *Trek* universe—both *Lower Decks* and *Strange New Worlds* are exactly what I love and would love to do more there."

IMDB lists her many accolades, but some stand out in her mind: "I have a Hugo award that is one of my prized possessions, despite it being almost impossible to get through an airport because it looks like a little missile. And I have an Inkpot award, which is awarded at ComicCon, and which I am extremely moved by. And I wrote for three of the WGA's 101 Best Written TV Series, which seems like a lot."

Espenson lives in Los Angeles but travels often. She includes Southern Australia among her favorite frequent destinations.

Have you always been into science fiction and fantasy? Or was there a transition point—a time or an event that shifted your interests?

I've always loved sci-fi and fantasy—definitely go-to genres during my youth. My childhood was full of a lot of *A Wrinkle in Time* and Narnia type books. There was a series of books by Edgar Eager, about kids having magic adventures, that I read and re-read many times. In one of the books, the protagonist kids glimpse the protagonists of one of the author's OTHER books in the middle of their adventure—a crossover that blew my tiny mind.

I loved *The Hobbit* but found *The Lord of the Rings* to be hard sledding—I was probably too young. Loved Ray Bradbury, loved *Dune*, loved books about magic and space adventures, though I feel that I generally liked those to be kept separate—I liked lots of science, not magic, in my science fiction. I bought lots of books just because there was a woman in a space suit on the cover; I pretty much was pulling books and stories off the shelf randomly, without a sense of what was considered schlock vs classic fare—which probably gave me a pretty good balanced diet.

What do you see as some of the most formative genre works for you, whether books or shows you came across, or something that left a lasting impression on you?

I came to *Star Trek* in an unusual way—I read the novels first. A lot of the early *Trek* novels were quite daring, with lots of revealing character moments and really fun speculative elements. These really made the *Trek* universe feel enormous, adult, and lived-in. I could imagine living on the Enterprise. These were a HUGE influence on me. I also love humor in my sci-fi, so there was a lot of Douglas Adams, and later, Jasper Fforde.

You've worked on some of the most iconic genre television shows. How would you describe the relationship between the television industry and the genre fiction industry, in terms of both novels and short stories?

I've written a number of things that began as novels—my episode of *Game of Thrones* comes to mind, of course. This was in season one, and the events followed what George R. R. Martin had written very closely. This was a fascinating experience—the opposite of taking a script and novelizing it. It was denovelization and I enjoyed it a lot. A scene in a novel can go on a long time without getting boring because you're inside the heads of the characters, accomplishing all kinds of things. Put all of that on the screen and it will feel too long—one scene generally accomplishes only a few things. So it was an exercise in finding the little crucial acorn at the heart of each scene.

I also once was tasked with turning a short story, in this case by Philip K. Dick, into a teleplay. Ultimately, it wasn't produced, but it was a fascinating process. In this case, the story would've provided only the concept, with all new characters populating it—totally different than the *Game of Thrones* situation.

In terms of the relationship going in the other direction, I was hoping that the show *Caprica* would provide opportunities for novels set in the world of the show. I loved those *Star Trek* novels of my childhood so much, and I wanted to create that same kind of feeling—that this was a boundless world. I met with a few novelists, some brought me ideas that excited me, but the show was both too all-consuming in terms of workload—and too short-lived—for these to ever get realized.

What do you see as some of the most important recent changes in the television industry, and do those changes ripple out to the book industry?

The most important recent changes to TV, in terms of how it affects the working life of writers, is that jobs tend not to involve nine months of full-time work, including being involved in the production of episodes.

Shorter seasons, spaced farther apart, and with less writer involvement during production means that writers work for shorter stints, and need to cobble together multiple projects to fill out their working schedule. So everyone is beating the bushes, looking for gigs, and of course, trying to create opportunities out of thin air.

To that end, I have heard that there is a current crop of *unpublished short stories* being purchased by Hollywood. In order to demonstrate the value of the projects they want to create, TV writers are writing prose stories . . . which those writers are then hired to develop into pilots and series. This bypasses the book industry, of course, unless authors (as opposed to TV writers) jump in to write those stories, instead of letting TV writers monopolize this path.

And by the way, maybe there should be a new thriving market for sci-fi anthologies. If these stories are compelling enough to turn into shows, then surely they're good enough to publish.

You have also written fiction. What are some of the most important differences for you between writing for television and writing fiction?

The big difference is obvious—in script writing, you only have dialogue. Once you have actors, of course, you will have another way to convey the internal experience of the characters, but before a script is produced, it's just dialogue and descriptions of actions. So you have to really think hard about all the different ways that internal states are revealed by how we speak. This is where I'm grateful for that background in linguistics—it taught me to really listen hard to how people actually speak and what they're doing when they choose their words and imagery.

It might seem as if writing prose would be freeing, because you can get the character's internal state straight from them, without figuring out how to bury it in their language. Exposition about relationships is so much easier when a character can just tell the reader that the person at the door is their sister with whom they have a troubled past. That's notoriously hard to convey in any detail when the scene just has the two characters talking—they're not going to talk about things they both already know. *But* I really love writing dialogue and usually prefer it. Oddly, I feel like I have to slow down to capture the internal stuff, when I'd rather just race ahead at speaking pace. I've discovered that when I'm writing a short story, it helps to deprive the main character of someone to talk to, to force myself to honor the internal.

When you look back on your extensive entries as a writer in visual media, what for you are a few of the things you worked on that you are most proud of, and what makes them stand out?

I love that I wrote for the season of *Ellen* after the character came out. That was pioneering television, and of course I'm really proud of the work I did on the *Buffy/Angel/Firefly* shows—they had the mixture of humor, message, and real depth that I love. And then I was startled and gratified to get the chance to work on a similarly complex and challenging project with *Battlestar Galactica*. It was fun and flattering to work on *Game of Thrones*, but it was only one episode as a sort of guest-writer, so it's hard to take credit for anything there. I worked on *Torchwood* (*Torchwood: Miracle Day*) and Marvel's *Jessica Jones* at around the same time, and they were both really rewarding as well. Two amazing showrunners: Russell Davies and Melissa Rosenberg—love them both. As a room experience, *Torchwood* was tumbling burbling fun, while *Jessica Jones* was focused and so productive—totally different, both creative, and I'd do either again in a heartbeat. Recently, I've been on the two Fs: *Foundation* and *Fallout*. Again, totally contrasting experiences that I've loved and where we've done work I really respect. I should also mention *Once Upon a Time*, where I worked for seven wonderful years, weaving fairytales—great fun with an amazing staff.

Overall, I'm very proud of how *many* "universes" I've been privileged to write for: Marvel (*Jessica Jones*), the *Buffy/Angel*-verse, *Star Trek*, *Star Wars* (the unproduced *Star Wars: Detours* series), the DC universe (the *Batman* animated series), *Doctor Who*niverse (*Torchwood*), and should we count *Game of Thrones* and *Battlestar Galactica* as universes as well? What should I add? Sherlock Holmes?! That would be fun!

Are there projects that you really wanted to make happen that just didn't happen for one reason or another?

I adore *Star Trek: Lower Decks* and REALLY wanted to write for that show, but it ended far too soon. I implore the powers that be to revive it—I will sign up instantly. I also would love to work on a show set in the golden age of Hollywood—I had a pitch for a show like this put together once, but it didn't happen. But ultimately, I don't want to *create* it, just write episodes. This is something that becomes clear in this career—being the creator of a show limits how much fun you get to have writing it . . . at least it looks like that to me! I like to move, hummingbird-like, from show to show.

Some of your work has involved bringing characters and ideas originally presented in print form into television, such as Jessica Jones, Foundation, and more. What are some of the most significant challenges of these kinds of projects, and what are some the most rewarding aspects?

In both those cases, I wasn't the one crafting the adaptation. And in both those cases the adaptation was such a thorough re-imagining that I primarily engaged with the show, not the source material. The show is its own world and the showrunner/creator has already made the choices about what belongs in the world. This is very different than, say, working on a *Star Trek* show, in which all the previous shows are something different than source material—they are also canon.

The only script I've written in which I was adapting directly from the source material was my episode of *Game of Thrones*—which was really fun because it was a totally new challenge for me.

The challenges of the *Jessica Jones* and *Foundation* kind of work don't really differ from writing for any show—you're trying to capture the voices and tone of the series overall, while trying to make everything feel grounded and compelling . . . all the usual things. In terms of special rewards—there is a great sense of accomplishment when the fans of the source material welcome it and recognize it as a legitimate part of what they love. But, again, I'm generally just a writer on these shows, not a creator, so that credit really goes to others.

What are the things that you really wish more people knew about the television industry or related fields?

I don't like it when I see individual writers given too much blame for a single moment or line of dialogue—so much of TV is written by the whole staff, or re-written by higher-level writers, or even changed on set! The same doesn't apply to giving the writer too much credit—that's fine. Bring it on.

What are your favorite bits of advice for writers who may have made their mark in writing fiction, but are interested in also writing for television or film?

This goes back to something I mentioned earlier—the enthusiasm for "existing IP" that has TV writers writing stories to establish IP that they then sell for themselves to write. I'd suggest that prose writers may want to put their minds to this same project: writing stories that would adapt well as the kind of shows that are being made now. Your representatives should be able to get a promising property into the hands of studio executives. If something gets purchased, you'll be teamed with someone who already has experience making television—and you can learn from them! I'm making it sound easy, of course, and it's anything but. We are all mystified about what sells and what doesn't, and there are gatekeepers everywhere. But if unpublished stories from TV writers are selling . . .

Is there anything else you'd like to share about you or your work, including anything recent or upcoming you'd love for people to check out?

I've been writing for a long enough time to become what I hoped to be: a journeyman writer. I never wanted to create and run my own shows; I always wanted to move from show to show, writing for many different kinds of characters, employing different tones, different genres. At its best, I think TV writing is like TV watching—you're dropped into the world. And what I've been doing is the equivalent of changing the channel, flipping through everything there is to offer. So far, a good career, and only half-way over!

ABOUT THE AUTHOR

Arley Sorg is an associate agent at kt literary. He is a two-time World Fantasy Award Finalist and a two-time Locus Award Finalist for his work as co-Editor-in-Chief at *Fantasy Magazine*. Arley is also a SFWA Solstice Award Recipient, a Space Cowboy Award Recipient, and a finalist for two Ignyte Awards. Arley is senior editor at *Locus*, associate editor at both *Lightspeed* & *Nightmare*, a columnist for *The Magazine of Fantasy and Science Fiction* and an interviewer for *Clarkesworld*.

Inside the Science Fiction Studio: A Conversation with David Barr Kirtley

ARLEY SORG

David Barr Kirtley was born in Philadelphia but his earliest memories are of Katonah, in northern Westchester, where he lived through high school. On his site, his parents are described as "two PhD scientists fond of books, the outdoors, travel, current events, and classical music" and he says that at a young age they read him things like "the novels of Robert Heinlein, Madeleine L'Engle, William Sleator, and J.R.R. Tolkien . . . Isaac Asimov and Larry Niven." Kirtley shared that his father studied physics "because he wanted to be a science fiction writer. He never ended up writing any fiction, but he did become a prominent physicist, working at IBM and Stanford and consulting on scanning SQUID microscopy at labs all over Europe." Early on, David Barr Kirtley was publishing short fiction in magazines that showcased student writing, such as *Merlyn's Pen*.

Kirtley went to Colby College in Maine for undergrad. During his first year, he won the Dell Magazines Award for Undergraduate Excellence in Science Fiction and Fantasy Writing with the story "Lest

We Forget." He earned a degree in Government, his studies focusing on Constitutional law and political philosophy, with a minor in Creative Writing. He moved to Somers (near Katonah), and then he went to the University of Southern California in Los Angeles for grad school, completing a Master of Professional Writing with a focus on fiction and screenwriting. Subsequently, he moved back to Somers. He also attended the Clarion workshop (when it was in Michigan), the Odyssey Workshop, the CSSF Workshop, Orson Scott Card's Literary Boot Camp, and Viable Paradise. Early landmark appearances include stories "The Disciple" in *Weird Tales* (Summer 2002) and "Seven Brothers, Cruel" in *Realms of Fantasy* (December 2002).

By 2010, a number of Kirtley's pieces had been rendered in podcast format. The experience had been transformative, as his site demonstrates: "I suggested to John [Joseph Adams] that we should release a podcast episode of the two of us chatting about *The Living Dead*, and that idea eventually mushroomed into us doing a weekly interview/talk show for Tor.com that we called *Geek's Guide to the Galaxy*, in honor of Douglas Adams." The show moved to *io9* for episodes 22 through 51, then to *Wired*. In December 2013 they had aired 100 episodes, and Adams stepped down as co-host—though he continued to appear as a regular guest.

That same year, Kirtley met Steph Grossman at a Karen Russell reading at the Center for Fiction. Three years later, they moved in together in Astoria. In 2019 they moved to Austin so that Grossman could earn her MFA in Creative Writing at Texas State University. "I proposed to Steph in 2021 on the road leading up to the ski basin in Santa Fe, a spot I picked because it's one of the locations featured in my favorite book series, *The Chronicles of Amber* by Roger Zelazny." They were married in 2023 at the Center for Fiction, in its new Brooklyn location, with Adams as Kirtley's best man, and numerous *Geek's Guide* regulars in attendance. Grossman landed a job as an assistant professor in the English department at Texas State, so they still live in Austin, along with daughter Taryn Amber Kirtley— "Amber is obviously a reference to *The Chronicles of Amber*, and we picked Taryn partly because it sounds sort of like 'Terran,' a name used for inhabitants of Earth in a lot of classic science fiction. Taryn was also born on August 29th, the date of Judgment Day in the *Terminator* movies."

Geek's Guide to the Galaxy has featured guests such as David Cronenberg, Felicia Day, Joyce Carol Oates, Brent Spiner, Neal Stephenson, and many others; writers, game designers, scientists, showrunners, and more. "For the past decade I was making a modest living as a full-time writer/podcaster, mostly thanks to our Patreon supporters and a partnership with *Wired.com* that ended last year. Currently I'm a stay-at-home dad and have scaled way back on how much time I'm able to devote to the podcast. I'm still trying to get an episode out every other week but I don't always make it."

According to your personal site, you have interviewed over four hundred guests, including folks whose names most people would recognize. Geek's Guide launched in 2010, so you've been working in that specific context for over fifteen years. What has changed about your approach to interviews over time and practice?

When I started the podcast (along with John Joseph Adams) I had no experience conducting interviews, but I did have a lot of experience attending book launches, where I would typically ask a bunch of questions during the Q&A session. (From 2000-2010 I probably attended hundreds of book events, often two to three per week.) I treated my early interviews as extended Q&A sessions, where I would draft a long list of questions beforehand and just reel them off one by one. My perspective at the time was that most interviewers were self-absorbed airheads who tended to monopolize the conversation with their own inane babble, often making it impossible for the guest to get a word in edgewise, and my goal was just to be as unobtrusive as possible. I also grew up at a time where fantasy & science fiction were widely derided, and I wanted my interviews to be really serious and thoughtful and help to push back against the perception of science fiction as frivolous. (I envisioned my interviews as something like *Inside the Actors Studio* or *Charlie Rose* for science fiction.)

Most listeners seemed to enjoy the interviews, but there was a vocal subset who constantly told me I was the worst interviewer they'd ever heard and that I had no personality, and my interviews lacked flow. I eventually decided they had a point, and tried to make my interviews more conversational, so now I always ask follow-up questions and try to refer to my list of questions as little as possible during the interview, and I also try to be a little more relaxed and humorous.

How has the function, shape, and the goals of the show changed since its inception back in 2010?

The original format of the show was that John Joseph Adams and I would interview a guest, and then he and I would chat about some related topic after the interview. For example, we would interview Robert Kirkman and then afterward John and I would talk about our favorite zombie movies. This worked well at the beginning, but after a while we started running out of topics that we were experts on. At that point we started bringing on "guest geeks" who could fill in any holes in our expertise, but it started becoming harder and harder to include John in those discussions, because it's hard to contribute much when you're on a panel with the world's biggest superfan of a particular topic. After a hundred episodes John decided to step back from his role as full-time co-host and only appear on panels that he had some special interest in.

Initially we were doing an episode every week, but as I got more experienced the episodes got longer and longer, and eventually I had to scale it back to every other week. At a certain point the interviews and panels were both over an hour long, at which point it made sense to split up the show and make each interview and panel its own episode. After that we went back to releasing episodes every week, a schedule I kept up for about ten years, but recently I scaled it back to every other week again after a very busy couple of years in which I got married, bought a house, and had a daughter.

In terms of the goals of the show, I always wanted it to be something that promoted science fiction and also promoted science and reason, two goals I always saw as inextricably linked. (Many of my favorite authors growing up such as Isaac Asimov and Douglas Adams always had a very strong pro-science, anti-superstition bent to their work.) I always wanted the show to be something like *Real Time with Bill Maher* or *The Daily Show* with Jon Stewart, except with it being "politics and science fiction" instead of "politics and comedy." But I really liked how those shows would have guests from across the political spectrum matching wits in a good-natured way, rather than just shouting at each other. (When I was a kid I would watch *Politically Incorrect* with Bill Maher, and occasionally they would have on an author like Harlan Ellison or Clive Barker, which thrilled me, and I always wanted more of that.) So those two goals were always really important to me: legitimizing and popularizing science fiction while also promoting science and skepticism.

These days our panels are mostly "book club" episodes, where we discuss a classic novel, "TV season reviews," where we review one or two seasons of a recent TV show, "new movie panels," where we do a deep dive on a recent movie, or "classic movie panels," where we discuss five classic movies. I was surprised to notice recently that we've done seventy-eight TV review episodes. I don't think of myself as watching that much TV—I mostly just do the TV review episodes because they're easy and because my friends are always enthusiastic about them—but I guess I do actually watch a lot of TV.

One recent format change I'm really excited about is that we've started doing deep dives into single author short story collections where we review every story in the book. This happened by accident. Back in Episode 475 my friend Tom Gerencer and I discussed Robert Sheckley's collection *Store of the Worlds*. We spent an hour discussing the book in some detail but didn't cover every single story. We had so much fun doing that that I decided to do it again with the new collection *The Best of Roger Zelazny*.

For that one Tom suggested we start with the stories we liked the least and progress to the ones we liked the best. I agreed, not fully realizing this meant we were committing ourselves to discuss every story in the book. It took us two and a half hours, but we did it. We followed that up with a four-hour discussion of the new book *Harlan Ellison's Greatest Hits*, split over two episodes. I really enjoyed those shows, and as far as I know no one else has provided such in-depth discussion of those books. Possibly a four-hour discussion of a short story collection is more detail than anyone really wants, and maybe no one will listen to them, but personally I love the format and am looking forward to doing more.

Has the show ever faced challenges and setbacks or has it been fairly smooth sailing from the get-go?

John and I started doing the show in partnership with *Tor.com* (now *Reactor*), and the closest the show ever came to ending was when that partnership ended after about five months. When we started, I had no idea how time-consuming doing a podcast would be, and I definitely wondered at that point if it was worth it. But after a five-month hiatus we struck up a new partnership agreement with *io9* (now part of *Gizmodo*), and over the next year or two I got to interview George R. R. Martin, Richard Dawkins, Ursula K. Le Guin, William Gibson, Orson Scott Card, Neil deGrasse Tyson, Simon Pegg, and China Miéville, and after that I was pretty much hooked.

The second most challenging time for the show is probably now. We had a partnership agreement with *Wired.com* which ended in March 2024 after thirteen years. In a way the timing worked out, because my daughter was born last year and I wouldn't have had time to keep writing articles for *Wired.com* anyway. (I wrote over 500 articles for *Wired.*

com summarizing each episode of the podcast, which was a fantastic opportunity but was also incredibly time-consuming. Each one took basically an entire day to write, so I figure I've devoted well over a year of my life just to writing those articles.)

The market conditions for doing a show like *Geek's Guide to the Galaxy* have also changed dramatically. When we started in 2010 there were only a handful of science fiction podcasts, and we were growing at a steady clip for a long time, but in 2025 the podcast space is glutted with content and it's almost impossible to stand out. We also benefited enormously from a period where "geek" stuff achieved a certain cultural cachet, but that trend seems to have peaked. Our rise also coincided with an era where crowdfunding was exciting and novel, and lots of niche projects attracted huge support, a trend that also seems to have peaked. I also think that Hollywood movies and TV shows have lost of lot of their luster—lots of sequels and prequels, lots of shows being canceled after one or two seasons, lots of shows hidden away on streaming services that no one watches—and the less enthusiasm there is for science fiction movies and TV shows, the less enthusiasm there will be for discussions of them. Then there's the fact that much of the podcasting audience has shifted over to YouTube, where the algorithm greatly favors those who pump out a daily stream of low-effort content, which is why the platform is dominated by twenty-minute videos of people talking into their cameras, a format that doesn't really appeal to me.

It's also challenging to keep a show like this going for more than fifteen years. At this point I've interviewed most of my favorite authors and discussed most of my favorite books and movies. I'm not interested in repeating myself, but there's also a point of diminishing returns as you delve into more and more obscure corners of the genre. (A review of *The Urth of the New Sun* is never going to get as many downloads as a review of *Dune* no matter how much effort you put into it.) It's fun to discover new authors, but in my busy adult life it's increasingly difficult for me to keep up with all the new authors or offer any sort of informed perspective on their work. (I used to consider myself an expert on all things fantasy & science fiction, but these days if I want to do an episode on "LitRPG" or "romantasy," I first have to figure out what the hell those things are.) It's also hard to maintain much momentum when you're only putting out two episodes a month—though maybe that'll change once our daughter is old enough to start daycare.

Speaking of that, another big challenge that's cropped up lately, now that my friends and I are all in our 40s and 50s, is just finding a time to record when everyone's available. Between jobs and kids and vacations, scheduling some of these panels can take months, and then everything can be thrown into chaos if one person didn't have time to read the book or has a last-minute conflict.

So yeah, there are a lot of challenges. I doubt I would ever shutter the show completely, because it's fun to be able to chat with my friends about movies and interview some of my favorite public figures, but I could definitely see myself spending less and less time on it over the next few years.

As of this writing, recent episodes include discussions of work by Gene Wolfe, Harlan Ellison, Roger Zelazny, Robert A. Heinlein, and others; film and television episode reviews; and author interviews or guest discussions, including Philip Gelatt, Melinda M. Snodgrass, and more. How do you decide what topics to cover, as well as who to invite onto the show?

When we first started out, I basically just wanted to interview my favorite authors, podcasters, and public intellectuals, so that's pretty much what we did. We also interviewed a lot of up-and-coming authors who John and I knew from the convention circuit, or authors that we weren't necessarily that familiar with but who would be well-known to our audience. I've also interviewed a lot of authors about their short story collections, which is fairly unusual, but I find that interviewing an author about a short story collection is far more interesting than interviewing them about a novel, because there's so much more to talk about and also because I just like short story collections more than novels. So for the first decade of the show, pretty much all I read were brand new books by whichever author I was planning to interview that week.

About five years ago the focus of the show shifted away from new books and movies and toward classic books and movies. This happened for a couple of reasons. One was that by that point I had already interviewed most of my favorite authors. Another was that I hadn't read any classic science fiction for almost a decade, and I was becoming increasingly self-conscious about the fact that I had never read *Dune*, *Foundation*, *Neuromancer*, *Snow Crash*, *The Left Hand of Darkness*, *Stranger in a Strange Land*, and a bunch of other classics that I had either missed completely or in some cases started but never finished. It seemed like a higher priority to read those rather than the latest release from a contemporary author that I was only somewhat familiar with.

Another reason for the shift was that my friend Andrea Kail started agitating for us to discuss "Bad '80s Movies." We did that in Episode

371, and it was so much fun that we turned it into a regular feature, though recently we've started branching out into '90s movies because we started running out of '80s movies we wanted to talk about.

One distinctive aspect of the show is that I've interviewed a lot of well-known public figures who you wouldn't necessarily expect to see on a science fiction podcast, people like Richard Dawkins, Amanda Knox, Andrew Yang, Steven Pinker, Margaret Atwood, Kazuo Ishiguro, Garry Kasparov, and Matthew Yglesias. Part of this is just that I think they'd be interesting to talk to, and part of it is my attempt to legitimize science fiction by getting high-profile guests on the show. Whenever I'm able to line up an interview with a high-profile guest, I always try to ask them about their interest in science fiction. Sometimes they flatly admit they don't know much about science fiction, but a surprising number of them are big fans. The Kazuo Ishiguro interview was one of our most popular episodes, because in a surprising twist Ishiguro was really curious about science fiction and spent the last twenty minutes of the interview questioning me about the genre.

Many authors are uncomfortable being interviewed; also, some folks can be generally more challenging in terms of just getting them talking. What are some of your techniques for dealing with those kinds of situations?

I haven't really had much of any issue with people being too quiet. In my experience bad interviews generally fall into two categories: 1) guests who ramble and 2) guests who deliver pre-rehearsed answers no matter what you ask. I did have one interview once that I had to scrap because the guest was too quiet (all of his answers were basically "Huh, that's a good question. I don't know"), but that's by far the exception.

I think the biggest thing you can do to make an interview successful is to ask questions that show that you're familiar with the guest's work, especially their recent work. Most author interviews are just generic questions that could apply to any writer ("Where do you get your ideas? Why do you write science fiction? Do you write by hand or on a computer?"). No one is going to be enthusiastic to get a bunch of questions like that. It's also a sad reality that many people are only famous for one thing, and everyone wants to talk to them about that one thing, but you can expect an air of weary resignation if all of your questions are about something the guest did forty years ago.

The second thing, as I mentioned above, is to ask follow-up questions and let the guest dictate the direction of the conversation. Sometimes they'll bring up something you weren't planning to talk about until later, but I've generally found it's better to just go with whatever they want to talk about and possibly circle back to your other questions later. (If you really don't want to get off track, you can say something like "Yeah I definitely want to get to that, but first just let me ask you about this.")

But again, the far bigger issue in my experience is guests who ramble on and on. I had one interview where I basically asked one question, and then the guest delivered a 45-minute monologue, free associating from topic to topic, then said, "Whoops, I've got to go. I really went on for a long time, didn't I? Well, that's your fault for not interrupting me. Bye." I'm a very polite person who finds it very difficult to interrupt people, and I used to figure it was better to just let guests drone on and on and then tighten up their answers in editing, but this often leads to interviews that don't sound natural and lack flow. Much as I hate to say it, if you're going to be a good interviewer you need to learn to interrupt people. One technique that might help, rather than doing a full interruption, is to start chiming in with a string of "Yeah . . . " and "Well . . . " and "But . . . " Hopefully the guest will take the hint and stop talking. If you do have to do a full interruption, I find something like "Well actually, let me ask you about that" works best.

Guests who deliver pre-rehearsed answers are even trickier. The best thing I've found is to get the guest talking about their feelings. So they may be giving you a bunch of rehearsed factual statements about their book, and you can say something like "What was it like when the book came out? Were you excited?" You always need to make the interview about the guest or else the conversation will feel lifeless. So if you're interviewing an expert on Julius Caesar, you can't just ask questions about Julius Caesar. You also need to ask stuff like: "How did you get interested in Julius Caesar? Did writing this book change how you feel about Julius Caesar? What do your friends and family think about your obsession with Julius Caesar?" Often it takes about twenty minutes for a guest to warm up to you, especially if they've been doing a lot of interviews and answering the same questions over and over. A twenty-minute warmup period can be okay in an hour-long interview but is definitely a problem in a twenty-minute interview, which is why I tend to avoid twenty-minute interviews.

At one point you reported to Locus that the show averaged twenty thousand unique visitors per month. Your Apple Podcasts platform has a 4.6-star rating with over fourteen hundred ratings; your YouTube channel boasts nearly forty-five hundred subscribers,

while individual episode views vary. Who do you see as the Geek's Guide audience? And what do you see as the overlap between the Geek's Guide audience and people who read magazines?

I think our core demographic is probably people like me who grew up loving fantasy & science fiction in the '80s and '90s, but I've heard from people of all ages and from all over the world who like the show. For a while we had more Facebook fans in Zagreb, Croatia than anywhere else on Earth. Especially in the early days when it was easier for people to randomly stumble across the show, I would hear from all sorts of people who weren't even science fiction fans who had started listening and were now getting into Gene Wolfe or Roger Zelazny, which was great. I think there's probably a fair amount of overlap between *Geek's Guide to the Galaxy* listeners and people who read magazines like *Lightspeed* and *Clarkesworld*. Many of our regular guests are contributors to those magazines, so many of those magazines get a free plug every time I read the bios at the start of the show.

For folks who haven't listened to the show but are now feeling curious, if you were to recommend maybe three episodes they should check out, what three would you want them to give a listen to, and why?

I think a good one to start with would be our panel on "Awesome '80s Fantasy Movies" back in Episode 486, where we discuss four classic fantasy movies—*The NeverEnding Story*, *Labyrinth*, *Ladyhawke*, and *The Princess Bride*. At the end of the episode, we also give our opinions on the five best fantasy movies of the '80s. These particular panelists—Andrea Kail, Matthew Kressel, and Tom Gerencer—have a really fun dynamic together, and if you enjoy the conversation there's a whole series of similar episodes to explore.

The next one I'll mention is our interview with Peter Watts, author of *Blindsight*, back in Episode 315. Peter is a fascinating, irascible character, and this long interview (almost two hours) ranges broadly from science to religion to politics, exploring such subjects as how he came to be banned from the U.S. and what inspired him to retell the story of *The Thing* from the point of view of the shape-shifting alien.

Finally, I'll mention our panel on "*Game of Thrones* Spoilers" back in Episode 146. In the early 2000s I was a massive fan of George R. R. Martin's fantasy series *A Song of Ice and Fire*. I spent hours a day on a George R. R. Martin message board, bought copies of *A Game of Thrones* and gave them out to anyone who would promise to read them, and transcribed the whole book by hand in order to get a taste of what it must have felt like to write it. All of my friends were similarly obsessed with the series, and this episode captures our anxiety and despair when it became clear that the TV adaptation was going to overtake and spoil the events of the books. I think this episode provides an interesting glimpse into a unique moment in geek history and also shows a bunch of hardcore fantasy fans at their most intense and passionate.

What do you wish more folks knew about podcasts?

I do wish more people appreciated how much work it takes to create a podcast like *Geek's Guide to the Galaxy*. I think for the average listener, the podcast just shows up in your feed each week and it seems sort of inevitable. It's just people talking into microphones and they sound like they're having a good time; how hard could it be? But you don't really think about all the time it takes to read all those books, watch all those shows, research all those topics, schedule all those recording sessions, and edit all that audio so that it sounds professional. I once read three books by a high-profile guest in preparation for an interview, and then in the end the guest just blew off the interview and all that time I'd spent getting ready was a complete waste. I know there's an endless buffet of content out there and it's impossible to support it all, but if there's something you really value please support it, because in the creative space most of the best stuff is somebody's passion project that they've made a lot of sacrifices to bring to life, and sooner or later they're going to have to throw in the towel and get a real job.

I also wish people understood just how amazing the podcasting space was in the early days, before it got invaded by comedians and celebrities and public radio personalities. There was a magical period from around 2004 to 2014 where the iTunes charts were dominated by all sorts of quirky, hyper-intellectual podcasts being produced by passionate hobbyists in their basements. It was a time when I was completely enraptured with podcasting and was getting into all sorts of niche shows that were completely outside the mainstream. These days the big podcasts all feel like the same sort of stuff you'd see on TV, which makes podcasting feel a lot less special.

You were also writing and selling fiction for a while, with publications spanning well over a decade. You published collection Save

***Me Plz and Other Stories* in 2022, which features twenty of your stories. Are you still writing fiction, or is it something that you have set aside?**

Yeah podcasting has definitely consumed most of my time over the past decade and hasn't left much room for anything else. I have noodled around with short fiction and had some TV writing gigs, but nothing that has really seen the light of day. I did spend pretty much every waking moment from the ages of twenty-one to thirty-two writing short fiction, and wrote over 100 short stories, so by the time podcasting came around I wasn't necessarily averse to trying something new. I really love writing short stories, but the process of publishing short stories is pretty unrewarding, with a single magazine often taking months to respond, and even when a story gets accepted it often takes months or years to actually appear. By contrast I can record a podcast and have it out that same week. Writing fiction also gets kind of lonely after a while, whereas podcasting keeps me in constant contact with many of my favorite people.

One of the biggest events that solidified my transition from short story writer to podcaster was the closing of *Realms of Fantasy* magazine. *Realms of Fantasy* was a beautiful, glossy magazine featuring full-color artwork for each story. It was on newsstands everywhere, even in my local supermarket, and had an active message board full of really great people. I had been reading the magazine since high school and had been submitting there for years, and I was just starting to become a regular contributor (I had five stories in *Realms of Fantasy* between 2002 and 2007) when the magazine closed abruptly in 2009, which was devastating for me. My understanding was that *Realms of Fantasy* was still profitable, just not profitable enough for the owners, who were not fantasy fans and had no real emotional stake in the magazine. That experience made me determined, when the opportunity to start my own podcast came along, to put everything I had into building a platform that I controlled and that could not be snatched away at any time.

I would like to get back to writing fiction someday, and I have a lot of story ideas I've written down over the years, but if I did I would probably want to focus on novels, because unfortunately there's just a very limited audience for short fiction. (When *Geek's Guide to the Galaxy* first started taking off, I used to fantasize that our tens of thousands of listeners would all buy my short story collections and allow me to make a living as a full-time short story writer, but that proved to be overly optimistic, to say the least.)

I do have endless pages of notes for an epic fantasy series I want to write someday, so that will probably be my next project. Its current title is *The Sword of Ontology* until a publisher inevitably makes me change it.

Is there anything else you'd like readers to know about you, your work or Geek's Guide to the Galaxy?

I guess I'll just plug my wife Steph Grossman, who is also a writer and podcaster. You should all go check out her horror podcast *Basement Girls*, which she hosts with her friend Bianca Perez. I appeared in Episode 12 to discuss the cartoon adaptation of Ray Bradbury's *The Halloween Tree*. There's also a scene in the recent horror movie *Lovely, Dark, and Deep* where the main character is listening to a bunch of podcasts, and two of the voices you hear are Steph and Bianca, so everyone should definitely go check that out as well.

ABOUT THE AUTHOR

Arley Sorg is an associate agent at kt literary. He is a two-time World Fantasy Award Finalist and a two-time Locus Award Finalist for his work as co-Editor-in-Chief at *Fantasy Magazine*. Arley is also a SFWA Solstice Award Recipient, a Space Cowboy Award Recipient, and a finalist for two Ignyte Awards. Arley is senior editor at *Locus*, associate editor at both *Lightspeed* & *Nightmare*, a columnist for *The Magazine of Fantasy and Science Fiction* and an interviewer for *Clarkesworld*.

Editor's Desk: From Unusual Places

NEIL CLARKE

This weekend, I returned to my college to drop in on their annual medieval festival and to see some alumni. Several of my friends were involved in the founding of this event and I was in attendance the first year. The second year, they brought me into the fold as a piece in a living chess game, where I fought and lost to another piece. I lived nearby and eventually worked for the university, so after graduation, I was invited to continue participating in the chess game for many years after. That granted me the privilege of seeing it evolve as each new class added their own stamp upon it.

Eventually, life took me in another direction and I ended my run as the longest-running character in the event's history. (Interesting fact: The only person who comes even close is Former NJ Governor Tom Kean, who was the university's president for fifteen years.) Several years passed before I started attending as a spectator, but it always had a special place in my heart. It's not the same, but I can still see the thread that carries through from the start. Driving home, I couldn't help but appreciate that it had endured and continued to find students—much like my friends and I—that have enjoyed being a part of it. Even though the approaches may differ at times, the passion is shared.

That's just like my colleagues that have published, are publishing, or will publish a genre magazine in the future. Despite our differences, of which there can be many, we all love short fiction and want to share those stories. It doesn't matter if they are professional or hobbyists, long-lived or gone after a single issue, or even respectable in the eyes of our community or not, that thread connects us. Of course, to best serve that common interest, you need to endure as That Medieval Thing (yes, that's its name) has done.

I often find inspiration in unusual places. Comparing magazines to a student club might be one of the odder paths I've taken, but the more I thought about it, the more it made sense. Clubs aren't businesses, but they are accustomed to existing on unsteady ground, even if they don't always recognize it. That unsteadiness comes in the form of year-in-year-out turnover in membership. It's a push and pull between tradition and new ideas/viewpoints. Sometimes, the past is entirely disregarded or forgotten and old mistakes made new again, but occasionally it works out fine because times have changed.

Most of the history of genre magazine publishing worked within a much more traditionalist mindset. There were best practices and constraints placed upon participation by the economics of print publishing and distribution. Small press magazines existed on the fringes, but had their own traditions as well. The arrival of online and digital magazines was a significant disruption that started changing how readers consumed fiction and created new avenues for those looking to enter the field.

The early days of online publishing were marked by a significant number of new magazines attempting to take advantage of the many opportunities the medium offered, but failing to find a way to make it work. Many tried to replicate the old standards only to discover that the universal laws were different. New approaches were tried and many of those failed as well. The new magazines that survived this period were both lucky and better at adapting. A new set of not-best-but-good-enough practices started to emerge for those in that bubble.

When ebooks emerged as a legitimate product, it changed things for both the online magazines and those that came before. Suddenly, an old way was viable in the new medium. This turned into a boon for those on both sides that were quick enough to recognize the value and had the ability to embrace it. Over the next few years, digital subscriptions became a stabilizing force in the economics of short fiction magazines, but not for everyone. Those who were slower to act, or arrived later, were shut out of some of the larger subscription platforms. Later, companies like Kickstarter and Patreon would provide them with alternatives. Over much of the same time, the bulk of marketing for magazines shifted to social media platforms, which offered a cheap way to reach a larger audience. Marketing simultaneously became more important as the number of publications outpaced the growth in the audience for short fiction.

Through this period, however, the business of magazines became more reliant on (or impacted by) a handful of corporations that did not share the same values. Amazon killed its subscription program and hid the subscriber lists from the publishers, leaving many of the larger publications (from online days and before) in a far more precarious state. Twitter, Facebook, and other social media platforms tweaked their algorithms to make unpaid marketing less effective and eventually started driving people to other platforms, fracturing the social media space. It wasn't all bad. For those that followed their readers to new platforms, there was an opportunity to broaden their reach. Against this backdrop, generative AI arrived and began messing with the submissions process for many publications and stealing their work to train new products.

The ground has been shifting with increasing frequency in recent years and it's been exhausting. *Clarkesworld* has never been on completely stable seas and I'm tired. Admittedly, the waves have been bigger than normal in recent years and dictating what we needed to focus on. The frustration some detected in my previous editorial is almost certainly connected to this. It's a distraction from the reason I'm doing all this, the thread. And that, right there, is why I'm finding inspiration in a student club. Despite a constant diet of change, they've endured by maintaining focus on their particular thread. It's their compass in a constantly shifting landscape and a way to find the joy in the work they do without worrying too much about their past baggage.

Just that little thought is already making the course a bit more clear to me, so score one for inspiration from unusual places. We intend to endure like they do. It's time to try a few things. Maybe even retry a few old ones.

ABOUT THE AUTHOR

Neil Clarke is the editor of *Clarkesworld Magazine, Forever Magazine,* and several anthologies, including the Best Science Fiction of the Year series. He is a three-time winner of the Hugo Award for Best Editor Short Form, the 2024 winner of the Locus Award for Best Editor, a four-time winner of the Chesley Award for Best Art Director, and a recipient of the Kate Wilhelm Solstice Award. His next anthology, *Best Science Fiction of the Year: Volume 8*, was published by Night Shade Books in September. He currently lives in NJ with his wife and two sons.

Jungleman II

COVER ART BY ARTHUR HAAS

ABOUT THE ARTIST

Arthur Haas is a concept artist from Amsterdam, the Netherlands. He specializes in environment design and concept art for the entertainment industry and has a passion for science fiction. Arthur works as a freelance artist for major Hollywood film studios and international book publishers, and sells original artworks online and in galleries.

Made in United States
Troutdale, OR
08/11/2025

33577001R00090